A Word from Stephanie
about Cheating

The whole thing started when I tried to help out a classmate. Super-cool cheerleader Lara was in big trouble. If she didn't pass our advanced social studies course, she'd get kicked off the cheerleading squad!

I'm one of the best students in class, and I do all sorts of extra-credit work for my teacher, Ms. Cropple. So, naturally, I told Lara I'd help her study.

Little did I know Lara's version of studying was cheating!

Lara told me her cousin had given her one of Ms. Cropple's old tests, and that we could use the test as a study sheet. Sounded like a good idea to me—until I found out the "study sheet" had the exact same questions on it as our next test!

I totally want to tell our teacher what happened. But Lara won't let me. She says telling the truth will get her kicked off the squad for sure! Now I need some good advice—fast!

Good thing there are plenty of people to ask for advice in my house. Right now there are nine people and a dog living there. And for all I know, someone new could move in at any time. There's me, my big sister, D.J., my little sister, Michelle,

and my dad, Danny. But that's just the beginning. When my mom died, Dad needed help. So he asked his old college buddy, Joey Gladstone, and my uncle Jesse to come live with us, to help take care of me and my sisters.

Back then, Uncle Jesse didn't know much about taking care of three little girls. He was more into rock 'n' roll. Joey didn't know anything about kids, either—but it sure was funny watching him learn!

Having Uncle Jesse and Joey around was like having three dads instead of one! But then something even better happened—Uncle Jesse fell in love. He married Rebecca Donaldson, Dad's co-host on his TV show, *Wake Up, San Francisco*. Aunt Becky's so nice—she's more like a big sister than an aunt.

Next, Uncle Jesse and Aunt Becky had twin baby boys. Their names are Nicky and Alex, and they are adorable!

I love being part of a big family. Still, things can get pretty crazy when you live in such a full house!

FULL HOUSE™: Stephanie novels

Phone Call from a Flamingo
The Boy-Oh-Boy Next Door
Twin Troubles
Hip Hop Till You Drop
Here Comes the Brand-New Me
The Secret's Out
Daddy's Not-So-Little Girl
P.S. Friends Forever
Getting Even with the Flamingoes
The Dude of My Dreams
Back-to-School Cool
Picture Me Famous
Two-for-One Christmas Fun
The Big Fix-up Mix-up
Ten Ways to Wreck a Date
Wish Upon a VCR
Doubles or Nothing
Sugar and Spice Advice
Never Trust a Flamingo
The Truth About Boys
Crazy About the Future
My Secret Secret Admirer
Blue Ribbon Christmas
The Story on Older Boys
My Three Weeks as a Spy
No Business Like Show Business
Mail-Order Brother
To Cheat or Not to Cheat

Club Stephanie:

#1 Fun, Sun, and Flamingoes
#2 Fireworks and Flamingoes
#3 Flamingo Revenge
#4 Too Many Flamingoes
#5 Friend or Flamingo?
#6 Flamingoes Overboard!

Available from MINSTREL Books

FULL HOUSE™
Stephanie

To Cheat or Not to Cheat

Devra Newberger Speregen

A Parachute Book

WORLDWIDE PUBLISHING™

A MINSTREL® BOOK

Published by POCKET BOOKS
New York   London   Toronto   Sydney   Tokyo   Singapore

A MINSTREL PAPERBACK *Original*

 A Minstrel Book published by
POCKET BOOKS, a division of Simon & Schuster Inc.
1230 Avenue of the Americas, New York, NY 10020

A PARACHUTE BOOK

 READING Copyright © and ™ 1998 by Warner Bros.

FULL HOUSE, characters, names and all related indicia are trademarks of Warner Bros. © 1998.

ISBN: 0-671-01727-6

First Minstrel Books printing November 1998

10 9 8 7 6 5 4 3 2 1

A MINSTREL BOOK and colophon are registered trademarks of Simon & Schuster Inc.

Cover photo by Schultz Photography

Printed in the U.S.A.

To Cheat or Not to Cheat

CHAPTER

1

◆ ◀ ▸ ◆

"He's sooo adorable! If our homework assignment was to give *him* a Native American name, I'd call him Boy With Cute Face." Stephanie Tanner giggled and tightened the scrunchie in her long, blond hair.

"Stephanie." Maura Potter laughed as she punched Stephanie lightly on the arm. "How silly."

Allie Taylor glanced up from her social studies book. "I think you've all *totally* lost it. Ms. Cropple's homework assignment was to pick Native American names for *ourselves*, not for the members of the high school football team."

Stephanie turned back to the social studies resource center's computer and continued typing a lesson plan for her advanced social studies teacher, Ms. Cropple.

"Well, I *love* talking about the high school football team," Stephanie told her friends over her shoulder.

"Especially when we're talking about *your* favorite player," Maura pointed out.

Darcy Powell spoke in a deep voice, pretending to be a stadium announcer. "Attention, ladies and gentlemen. Now taking the field, number twenty-three, quarterback Mark Votto!"

Stephanie giggled again. In fact, whenever she thought of Mark Votto, she couldn't *stop* giggling.

She remembered when the announcer at the high school stadium said those very words and she got her first glimpse of him.

It was the past weekend at the high school homecoming game. Stephanie could picture Mark trotting to the sidelines, removing his helmet, and wiping the sweat from his forehead. His golden-blond hair gleamed in the early afternoon sun.

She could picture him laughing with his teammates, making the dimples in his cheeks even deeper and more adorable.

"Earth to Stephanie!" Darcy called. "Hey, Ms.

Social Studies Aide, do you realize you haven't typed anything in the last five minutes?"

Stephanie shook her head. *What am I doing? I have to finish Ms. Cropple's lesson plan before this period is over.* She tapped away furiously at the keyboard.

Signing up as a social studies aide was one of the best ideas Stephanie had ever had. On one or two of her free periods every week, Stephanie typed up Ms. Cropple's lesson plans or graded some homework assignments. For her trouble, she got extra credit in Ms. Cropple's class. Occasionally, she got to hang out with the youngest, coolest, best teacher in the school—Ms. Cropple.

Maura scribbled something in her notebook. She pushed her small, round-framed glasses up on her nose. "The best Native American name I can come up with for myself is Likes to Write, but that is way too boring," she said, and sighed.

Darcy stood and stretched her long arms and legs. Stephanie always admired her graceful, athletic figure. She thought Darcy looked like a cross between Whitney Houston and Cheryl Swoopes. "This assignment is *so* wacky," Darcy observed.

"It *is* wacky," Allie agreed. "But so is Ms. Cropple's whole class." She twisted her light brown hair around her finger. "Who would have thought that advanced social studies could be this much fun?"

"Not me," Stephanie admitted. "I figured that since we were having class with students from the high school, we'd have to act completely serious. But Ms. Cropple makes everything totally casual and fun. I think it helps keep everyone interested."

Stephanie felt so lucky to be chosen for the first advanced class that combined middle school kids with students from the high school next door.

Maura, Allie, and Darcy were chosen for the course, too. They were in a different class from Stephanie, but they could still help one another with research and assignments.

"The best thing about Ms. Cropple's class is getting to hang with older kids," Darcy asserted. "Before the advanced course started, the high school kids didn't want to be bothered with the kids from the middle school. Now we're welcome at things like the homecoming game. If we play our cards right, maybe one of us will even be dating a high school guy, like a football player, by the end of the year."

"Honestly, Darce." Allie frowned. "Between you and Stephanie, I don't know who's more obsessed with the football team."

4

Stephanie noticed a slight blush creeping across Darcy's face. "Well," Darcy explained. "I *would* like to hang out with some older, more mature guys for a change. What's wrong with that?"

"I wouldn't hold my breath," Allie pointed out. "Mark and the entire football team only hang out with Lara Tempkin and the rest of the cheerleading squad."

"Yeah," Stephanie agreed. "And since we're not high school cheerleaders, and we don't have any *friends* who are cheerleaders, I don't think we stand much of a chance of getting near any of *those* guys."

The door to the resource room banged open. Ms. Cropple hurried in, carrying an armload of books and paper-stuffed folders.

"Hey, Steph," Ms. Cropple said cheerfully. "Allie . . . Darcy . . . Maura. How are my lesson plans going?"

"Pretty well, Ms. C," Stephanie answered. "Except I didn't know if I should double-check your spelling of the tribe names."

Ms. Cropple tossed a large book to Stephanie. Stephanie caught it with one hand. She glanced at the title. "*Native America*," she read out loud.

"I'd appreciate your checking them all. Sometimes I get lazy and don't look them up. That's the definitive dictionary of Native American words," Ms. Cropple explained. She walked over to the computer. "I should use it all the time," she added. "Those tribe names can be really tricky."

"Okay, Ms. C." Stephanie smiled at her teacher.

Ms. Cropple shoved her books and folders into her bookcase, then picked up a new stack of books from the top of her desk. She sighed, pushed her long, brown curls behind her ears, and smiled at the girls.

"Well, sorry, but I've got to run," Ms. Cropple told them. "I'm teaching my sixth period class outdoors today, and I want to go outside early and set up some stuff."

The girls all stared at her in amazement.

"Class *outside?*" Stephanie asked. "How come?"

Ms. Cropple smiled mysteriously. "Can't tell you. I'm teaching *your* class outside tomorrow, and I don't want to spoil the surprise." She raised her eyebrows at the group.

"Cool!" Stephanie exclaimed. She couldn't wait to see what her teacher had planned.

"So, anyway, thanks for typing up my lesson plans," Ms. Cropple said. She reached into her closet and pulled out a large bag. "Some props for today's class," she said, heading out the door. "See you all later."

Stephanie tossed *Native America* to Allie. "You guys look up the tribe names and call out the spellings," she instructed. "Then I can have this finished in no time."

"Okay, what's the first word—" Darcy asked.

Wham! The door to the resource room swung open again.

Stephanie turned—and froze.

She felt her heart beating in her throat. She gulped to try to stop it.

"Stephanie!" Allie whispered. "Do you see who's here?"

Stephanie nodded but could say nothing. She saw who was there, all right. She couldn't have missed him.

Not five feet away was quarterback Mark Votto!

Stephanie's hands flew up to her head. She pulled the scrunchie from her long, blond hair. "What's he doing here?" she asked when she was finally able to speak.

A large group followed Mark inside the resource center.

"What are they *all* doing here?" Darcy wondered. "Every single one of those people is from the high school. And they're all either on the cheerleading squad or the football team, aren't they?"

Stephanie nodded. "Yeah, and there's Lara Tempkin." She pointed to a girl with ultra-long, ultra-shiny light blond hair. She wore a form-fitting, fuzzy sweater that showed off her curvy figure. "She's in my social studies class."

The girls watched as Lara, Mark, and their friends tacked colorful flyers up around the middle school resource room. They were all goofing off, making a ton of noise.

"Must be nice to be a cheerleader," Allie commented in a whisper.

"Yuck!" Maura replied. "Being perky all the time isn't my style."

At that exact moment Stephanie could imagine it being *her* style. She stared at Mark's face—his cute, dimpled face—as he joked around with Lara Tempkin. She imagined herself standing in between them. Being friends with one of the coolest girls in the high school, and maybe—she almost gasped—going out with the most popular *guy* in the high school.

How awesome! She could be super popular in high school, before she even got there.

Stephanie shook her head, forcing herself out of her daydream. "The chances of us getting into that group are about a million to one," she told her friends. "None of them even know we exist—least of all, Mark Votto or Lara Tempkin—"

"Stephanie Tanner," someone called from across the room.

Stephanie swiveled around. Lara Tempkin was waving to her.

"Hey, Stephanie," Lara said. "You're just the person I was looking for!"

"Stephanie, *Lara Tempkin* is walking over here to talk to you!" Darcy squealed. "Be cool. This could be our ticket into the high school crowd."

CHAPTER
2

◆ ◂ ◼ ◆

Lara smiled as she walked over to Stephanie's computer desk. "Hey, Steph."

Stephanie knew Darcy was right. She had to stay cool. "Uh—hey. What's up?" Stephanie asked.

"Not much," Lara began. "We just came over to the middle school to tack up flyers about our pep rally. . . ."

Stephanie gazed over Lara's shoulder at Mark. He looked so gorgeous in his varsity letter jacket and jeans. She knew Lara was speaking to her, but all she could hear was a droning sound. She couldn't focus on anything but Mark.

"Stephanie!" Lara called loudly. Startled, Stephanie's eyes locked on Lara's.

"What? Huh?" Stephanie asked.

Lara giggled. "I was just asking you what *you* were doing in the resource center." She glanced at the computer screen.

"Oh, I'm doing some extra-credit work for Ms. Cropple," Stephanie told her.

"Get out of here," Lara said. "You can do that?"

Stephanie felt her gaze stealing back toward Mark. *Come on, focus,* she coached herself. *Even if Mark is standing right behind Lara, that's no reason to be rude. Especially if you want Lara to like you.*

"Anybody can get extra-credit work from Ms. Cropple," Stephanie informed her. "You just have to help her out."

"Doing *what?*" Lara asked.

"You know, typing lessons, grading papers, doing filing. Things like that," Stephanie explained.

"Wow!" Lara's eyes lit up. "You do all that? Then you really have the inside scoop when it comes to Cropple's class, don't you? Like, you know what we'll be learning ahead of time—and what kind of tests Cropple will be giving—and when she's springing a pop quiz."

"I don't know much about the quizzes, but I

do know the other stuff, I guess," Stephanie admitted.

"When do you find time to help Cropple?" Lara asked.

"During free periods," Stephanie explained.

Lara frowned. "Oh. I have cheerleading practice so often that my free periods are, like, the *only* time I get to hang out. Guess I won't be getting any extra credit."

Maura rolled her eyes. Stephanie knew what her friend was thinking. If Lara really wanted extra credit, she'd *find* time to help Ms. Cropple. But she couldn't say that to Lara.

Instead, Stephanie nodded sympathetically.

"*You* probably don't even *need* extra credit," Lara said. "You are a complete genius in class. You always know the right answers."

"Well . . ." Stephanie felt her face flush. She was embarrassed by the compliment. "I don't *always* know the right answer. But I do like hanging out with Ms. Cropple. She's awesome."

"Well, my grades are the total opposite of awesome," Lara went on. She perched on the edge of Ms. Cropple's desk. "So, are you in any clubs?" she asked, suddenly changing the subject.

Stephanie nodded. "Yeah, a few," she replied.

"Uh, Lara, you mentioned that you were looking for me . . ." Stephanie prompted.

Lara's eyes sparkled. "Oh, right!" she said. "I am! I mean, I was."

"How come?" Stephanie asked.

Lara's expression suddenly turned serious. "Okay, here's the thing," she said. "I'm, like, totally lost in social studies lately. I mean, with all my new duties as co-captain of the cheerleading squad . . . I'm *chapters* behind."

"Uh—we haven't really been following the social studies textbook closely anyway," Stephanie told her. "Ms. Cropple is doing this seminar thing on Native Americans and—"

"See?" Lara interrupted. "I didn't even know that! *That's* how far behind I am in class."

"But we've been learning about Native Americans for two weeks," Stephanie told her.

Lara laughed. "Well, I know *that*," she said, "I just didn't realize Ms. Cropple was doing this whole seminar thing. Anyway, about the class," she went on, "I knew you were super smart in it, but I had no idea how in touch you were with the whole social studies thing." She paused. "Basically, I was wondering if you could, like, do me this *huge* favor."

Stephanie frowned. What could she possibly do for Lara?

"Maybe the next time we have a take-home quiz, we can pair up or something to work on it?" Lara asked. "I could really use the help."

Stephanie glanced over at Darcy, Allie, and Maura. The three of them had been listening to Stephanie and Lara's conversation attentively. Allie caught her eye and shook her head slightly, as if to say, No, you can't do that!

Right next to Allie, though, Darcy had a happy, expectant look on her face. She gave Stephanie a thumbs-up. "Go for it!" she mouthed.

"I—I don't know, Lara," Stephanie said slowly. "I mean, we're supposed to work by ourselves on take-home quizzes."

"Oh, I know," Lara said. "I don't want you to give me the answers or anything. I just need some *help* with the studying—some *guidance*—that's all. For some reason, I don't seem to do well on Cropple's tests."

"Maybe it's because she spends all her free periods hanging out instead of studying," Stephanie heard Maura whisper to Allie.

"Lara, I'm not sure—" Stephanie began.

"Please?" Lara was practically begging. "I really need help! And you're, like, the absolute best person to help me!"

What do I do? Stephanie wondered. *Pairing up*

on a take-home quiz seems so wrong—but on the other hand, Lara seems so desperate.

"Lara, you coming?" a boy's voice suddenly called out. Stephanie whirled around and stood face-to-face with Mark Votto.

His nose was inches from her own. She could smell the wonderful scent of his cologne. None of the middle school boys wore cologne. Stephanie sucked in her breath. If she wanted to, she realized, she could tilt her head up and kiss him—

"Whoa! Sorry about that." Mark took a few steps back. "I guess I didn't expect you to turn around." He stood next to Lara.

Stephanie sighed. *That was totally intense.*

"Just a sec, Mark," Lara told him. "So, Stephanie . . . what do you say? It would really, really help me so much. And you could come hang out with me and all my friends." She put a hand on Mark's shoulder.

Mark, Stephanie realized, was one of the friends Lara was promising she could hang out with.

"Come on, it'll be fun," Lara insisted.

Stephanie hesitated. She glanced at her friends.

"Do it!" Darcy mouthed.

"Wait a minute," Mark said. "What are you asking for help in, Lara?"

"Stephanie Tanner here is going to tutor me in social studies," Lara told Mark.

"Wow! You're a tutor—uh, Stephanie, right?" Mark asked.

Stephanie felt her throat go dry. Wow! Mark was totally cute!

"Well, not exactly," Stephanie answered, giving him a small smile.

"But you're going to help Lara?" Mark asked. "That is so nice of you."

"Thank you. I—" Stephanie began.

"Great," Lara cried out. "It's all settled. I can't thank you enough for agreeing to help me!"

Wait! Stephanie thought. *When did I agree to that?*

"Uh, Lara, I still don't—" Stephanie tried again.

"I didn't know the girls in the middle school were so sweet," Mark said. He smiled.

She smiled back. *Yes! Mark thinks I'm sweet. It's only because he thinks I'm helping Lara, but there's no way I'm going to let him think otherwise now.*

"Yeah, well, we middle school girls like to help out," she replied.

Lara gave Stephanie a hug. "Stephanie, you're

cooler than cool. Thank you so much! I guess I'll see you on Thursday for the take-home, then. How about if I come over to your house?"

Stephanie's smile felt frozen to her face. She wished she could stop and say, *Wait, hold everything! I didn't mean to agree to help you with the quiz.*

She didn't want to ruin what Mark thought about her, though.

Lara and Mark turned and walked out of the resource center. "I'll catch you later, Stephanie!" Lara called over her shoulder.

"Yeah. See you," Mark said.

"Uh-huh," Stephanie replied weakly. She watched as Lara's entire crowd left the room.

"How perfect was *that?*" Darcy cried.

Stephanie looked up in confusion. "What are you talking about?" she asked in amazement.

"What am I talking about?" Darcy exclaimed. "You just got yourself in with *the* high school crowd. Complete with some of the coolest guys around!"

Stephanie stared at her. *I hadn't really thought about it that way,* she realized.

"Just think, Stephanie," Darcy went on. "You're in with Lara Tempkin! That means in a little while you can get us in, too!"

"I don't know," Allie said suddenly. "There

was something kind of *suspicious* about the way Lara acted just now. Don't you think?"

"What was suspicious?" Darcy asked.

"Well, for starters," Maura began, "Lara totally ignored the three of us."

"And she sure was interested in finding out exactly what kind of work you do for Ms. Cropple," Allie added. "She was acting *so* buddy-buddy with you. Why?"

"You heard her," Darcy pointed out, "she's doing poorly in social studies. So she asked how Steph gets extra credit. Then she asked Steph for study help. What's the big deal?"

"Also, why did she ask *Stephanie?*" Allie put in. "There must be someone in her crowd who's doing well in social studies. Why you, Steph?"

"Well, I *am* one of the smartest kids in my class," Stephanie said. "Lara just said so."

"Yeah," Darcy chimed in. "Maybe that's why. But really, *who cares* about why? Steph just found us a ticket to a brand-new group of friends. Cool friends. Older friends. And we were just saying we'd like to branch out a bit—weren't we?"

"It's true. We were," Stephanie admitted. "But Lara just asked me to help her with a take-home quiz. She didn't actually invite me to hang out. At least, not yet."

"So are you really going to do it?" Allie asked. "Are you going to help Lara with the quiz?"

Stephanie sighed. "It's not like I really have a choice in the matter," she replied. "I pretty much said I would. Even if I didn't mean to."

Loosen up, Stephanie, she told herself. *It's just one take-home quiz. What's the worst thing that could happen from helping Lara with one little quiz?*

CHAPTER

3

◆ ◂ ▪ ◆

Stephanie's stomach growled loudly.

She glanced at the alarm clock by her bed.
Dinner was just twenty minutes away. Good
thing, she realized. I'm starving!

She turned the page in her social studies book
and found a huge picture portraying an Apache
feast. Her stomach growled again. *Ugh!* Stephanie closed her book with a thump.

The bedroom door creaked open. Stephanie's
younger sister, Michelle, tiptoed into the room
they shared.

"Rock-a-bye, Flourie, on the treetop . . ." Michelle began singing.

Stephanie glanced up from her book.

"What are you doing?" Stephanie asked.

Michelle held a finger to her lips as she cradled a small bundle in her arms. "Shhh!" she whispered harshly. "I just got her to fall asleep!"

Stephanie's eyes widened. "You just got *who* to fall asleep?" she asked.

"Shhh!" Michelle ordered again. "You'll wake her up!"

Stephanie bolted upright. "I'll wake *who* up?" she demanded loudly. "Michelle, is that one of your dolls?"

Michelle rolled her eyes. "No, it's not a doll," she replied. "It's Flourie."

"*Who?*" Stephanie asked again.

Stephanie watched as her nine-year-old sister gently laid the bundle on her bed. Then she reached under the bed and pulled out a carton.

"Michelle, tell me. *Who* is *Flourie?*" Stephanie ordered. When Michelle didn't answer, Stephanie jumped off her bed. She marched over to her sister. "Is that a kitten or something? Does Dad know about this?"

"It's not a kitten," Michelle insisted. Stephanie watched as Michelle began to unwrap the tiny bundle.

"Then, who—" Stephanie stopped. She couldn't believe what she saw under the blanket.

"Flourie" was a sack of flour.

"Michelle!" Stephanie laughed. "You're using a sack of flour as a baby doll? Have you totally lost it?"

Michelle ignored her. She opened the carton from underneath the bed and pulled out a container of baby powder, some baby wipes, and a disposable diaper.

"You're diapering the flour?" Stephanie cried out in amazement. She burst into another fit of laughter.

"That's right," Michelle said finally. "And I wish you would keep your voice down, Stephanie. You already woke her up from her nap." Michelle leaned over and began to soothe the sack of flour.

Stephanie bit her tongue to keep from laughing again. Then she folded her arms across her chest. "Okay, Michelle," she demanded. "What gives? Are you trying to get Dad to buy you a new doll or something?"

"No!" Michelle replied. "Flourie is better than a doll. She's my school project for the next two weeks."

Stephanie watched, confused, as Michelle wiped, powdered, then taped a clean diaper onto Flourie.

"Hey, you did that pretty well," Stephanie told her sister.

"Thanks. Here, hold this for a minute?" Michelle asked. She handed Stephanie the diaper she had just taken off Flourie.

"Ew, yuck! No way!" Stephanie said in disgust. Then she stopped herself. "Wait—what am I saying? This isn't a *real* dirty diaper!" She crumpled it up and tossed it into the trash.

"So what's this project about, anyway?" she asked.

Michelle wrapped Flourie back in her blankets, then cradled her in her arms. "We all got flour sacks and baby supplies at school today," she explained. "For two weeks, we're supposed to pretend they're real babies. We have to love them and take care of them."

"How do you take care of a flour sack?" Stephanie asked.

"I told you. Like a real baby," Michelle insisted. "I have a chart over my desk," she said. "It tells me all the things I have to do to take care of Flourie. Isn't that right, Flourie?" she added, cooing to the flour sack in her arms.

Stephanie strode over to the chart on the wall. Five diaper changes a day . . . feedings at three in the morning . . . *playtime* . . . this was crazy!

"Michelle, are you really going to get up at

three o'clock in the morning to give a pretend bottle to a pretend baby?"

Michelle nodded. "Yup. I wouldn't want little Flourie to get hungry or sick or anything, right, little Flourie? Little sweetie-pie?"

"Ha-ha! Sweetie *pie!*" Stephanie exclaimed. "That's funny! Because you need *flour* to make a *pie*, right?"

Michelle glared at her. Stephanie stopped cold. Her sister couldn't be serious about taking care of a sack of flour—could she?

"You *were* trying to be funny, weren't you?" Stephanie asked.

"No. I wasn't," Michelle stated. She grabbed a baby rattle from the carton and headed for the door. "You can make jokes, Stephanie," she said. "But it's really important that I take the best care of Flourie. Especially if I want to win the Best Parent award in my class!"

She headed toward the door, shaking the rattle in front of Flourie. "Now, don't you let that mean lady upset you, my little sweetie-pie, er, I mean my little dumpling."

"Dumplings are made from flour, too," Stephanie yelled after her. Michelle didn't answer.

"Stephanie!" Danny called from the kitchen. "Telephone for you!"

It must be Allie, Stephanie thought. She ran

24

downstairs and into the living room. "I've got it!" she called to her father.

When she was sure her dad had hung up, Stephanie flopped down on the sofa.

"Allie!" she said. "Guess what Michelle is—"

Stephanie heard a giggle from the other end. "What's so funny?" she asked.

"Uh, this isn't Allie, Stephanie," the voice on the other end said. "It's me, Lara."

"Lara?" Stephanie asked.

"Yeah. I hope it's okay that I called."

"Oh, yeah, sure. I mean, I'm just surprised that's all," Stephanie responded. "How did you get my number?"

"It's right here on Ms. Cropple's contact sheet," Lara explained.

"Oh," Stephanie said. That made sense. Her social studies teacher gave each student a contact sheet at the beginning of the year. It had everyone's phone number on it, in case someone missed a lesson and needed to get notes.

"So, what's up?" Lara asked.

Stephanie settled back into the sofa. Wow! she thought. Lara called me just to chat. She is interested in being friendly.

Allie and Maura were obviously wrong. There was nothing suspicious about how Lara had approached her that afternoon.

"Not much is up, really," Stephanie told her. "I was just reading some stuff on Native American customs."

"You mean we had social studies homework tonight?" Lara asked. Her voice sounded nervous.

"Oh, no," Stephanie assured her. "I was just reading until dinner."

"I can't believe you, Stephanie," Lara said. "You're doing homework we don't even have. No wonder you're so smart."

"I'm reading ahead only because I like history," Stephanie explained. "Believe me, if I was *really* smart, I'd be reading ahead in science. I feel totally lost in that class!"

She paused a moment. "So, what's up with you?" she asked.

"Well, I just got home from cheerleading practice," Lara told her. "I'm going to grab some dinner, then meet some friends at the mall. You know, some of the other girls on the squad and a few guys from the team. Like Mark, the guy you met today—and a few of his friends. We hang out there every night.

"That's really why I was calling," she added. "I wanted to see if you were up for hanging out with us tonight."

Stephanie pictured herself at the food court

with Lara and Mark and their crowd. Their older crowd. Their popular crowd.

Then she pictured herself and Mark, wandering off alone together and having a private conversation. Maybe finding out that they liked each other. . . .

"Uh, Stephanie?" a voice broke through her daydream.

Stephanie shook her head. Yikes! She was still on the phone with Lara, and she hadn't been listening to her at all! "Oh, uh, sorry, Lara," she said, covering. "I thought my father was calling me."

"So do you want to come to the mall?" Lara asked again.

"Definitely! I'll meet you there."

"Excellent!" Lara said. "We usually hang out by the bagel stand at the edge of the food court. We'll be there around seven."

"Okay. See you," Stephanie said, and hung up the phone.

Yes! Her heart leapt. She was going to see Mark Votto tonight! She practically skipped back toward the stairs. Then, on the first step, she stopped mid-skip.

"Oh, no! I'm supposed to hang out with Darcy and Maura at Allie's house tonight," she remembered.

They were going to check out the new fashion Web site Allie found.

Stephanie hurried back into the living room and quickly dialed Allie's number.

"Are you mad?" she asked after explaining that she wanted to back out of their plans.

Allie sighed. "No, I'm not mad. How could I be mad? *I'd* rather hang out with Mark Votto, too."

"Thanks, Al! You're the best!" Stephanie told her friend.

"Yeah, yeah, yeah," Allie replied. "Well, don't go forgetting about us when you're the most popular girl at school. Boy, Darcy is going to be so jealous when she hears!"

Stephanie promised to fill them in the next day at their usual morning meeting spot—the pay phone outside the cafeteria.

"Get to school early," Allie ordered her. "So you can tell us everything!"

Stephanie hung up the phone and ran back up to her room. She was so excited, she felt like bouncing up and down on her bed.

It seemed like her dreams were all coming true—starting that night!

CHAPTER

4

♦ ◂ ◆ ♦

"Thanks for the ride, Dad," Stephanie said as they pulled up to the mall entrance.

"No problem, honey," Danny Tanner replied. "Are you sure you'll be able to get the social studies book you need at this bookstore?"

"Yep," Stephanie told her father. "Ms. Cropple told me I could find it here."

"Okay," Danny said. "Do you have enough money?"

"Absolutely." Stephanie checked her reflection in the vanity mirror above the passenger seat.

Lip gloss? Perfect. Hair? Perfect. Okay, Steph, you're ready to go, she told herself.

She gave her dad a good-bye peck on the cheek and climbed out of the car.

"Stephanie, hold on!" Danny called. Stephanie whirled around to face him. "Do you want me to wait for you?" he asked.

"Uh—that's okay, Dad," Stephanie covered. "I'm meeting a few of the kids from my class here, and we might decide to get a soda. I'm sure I can get a ride home from one of them."

Danny frowned. "I didn't know you were planning on hanging out on a school night." His face softened. "Well, just this once. I'll expect you home by nine-thirty—at the latest."

"Okay, Dad," Stephanie agreed. She pulled the door handle and leapt out of the car.

Stephanie smiled as she entered the mall. She *did* intend to buy a social studies book—one from Ms. Cropple's suggested reading list. When her father heard that, he was more than happy to drive her to the mall.

I can take a shortcut through Lane's Department Store, she realized, *and get to the food court in half the time*. She breezed through the second floor of the store and jogged down the escalator to the first floor of Lane's.

Nearly there, just one last look in the mirror. Stephanie stopped at a mirror at a cosmetics counter. She took off her jacket and quickly glanced around.

She gazed happily at her reflection. Her outfit was perfect. A soft red chenille sweater with black boot-cut pants.

"Can I help you, miss?" a voice suddenly asked.

Stephanie spun to her left and found herself face-to-face with a grim-looking salesperson.

"Oh, no, thanks," she replied. She could feel her face turn a million shades of red. "I was just . . . uh—never mind."

She grabbed her black mini backpack off the floor and strolled out of Lane's.

Stephanie found Lara exactly where she said she'd be, in front of the bagel stand. She was sitting on the edge of the mall fountain with three other girls Stephanie vaguely recognized.

Two guys sat with them.

Football players.

Stephanie could tell by their broad shoulders and strong builds.

One of the boys turned. Stephanie caught her breath. Mark Votto. He was there!

She squared her shoulders and strode confidently toward the group.

"Hi," she said cheerfully.

"Steph!" Lara cried. She jumped up and gave Stephanie a big hug.

Whoa! I know cheerleaders have spirit, she thought, *but I didn't know they were this spirited all the time!*

I can't believe she's hugging me. We're hardly what you would call close friends.

"Stephanie," Lara said, "this is Caryn Sawyer, Debbie DiAngelo, and June Segal. They're on the squad with me."

Stephanie smiled at the high school girls. All three of them wore boot-cut jeans and sweaters. Stephanie was secretly pleased—she'd made the right outfit choice.

"Hi," she responded.

"And, Steph, I think you know Mark," Lara went on.

Stephanie felt her heart beating triple-time. *Do I ever,* she thought.

She took a deep breath and ordered herself to remain cool. "Hey," she said to him.

"Hey." Mark returned her greeting and smiled. Stephanie thought she would melt from his dazzling grin.

"And this is Brett Johnson," he said. "He's on the team with me. Brett, this is Stephanie Tanner."

Stephanie smiled. Brett flashed a smile back. He seemed so nice! And friendly, too.

"So, Stephanie, tell us *all* about yourself. You write for the middle school newspaper, right?" Caryn asked abruptly.

She cleared her throat. *"The Scribe?* Yeah. Actually, it's one of my favorite things to do," she answered.

"Do you want to be a journalist someday?" Mark asked.

"It sure seems that way," Lara told everyone. "Not only does Stephanie write for *The Scribe,* she's also the producer for *Scribe TV."*

"Whoa!" Stephanie said. "I didn't realize you knew so much about me, Lara."

"Let's just say I did my homework," Lara replied.

"What's *Scribe TV?"* Debbie asked.

"It's a TV news program that airs in our homerooms every morning," Stephanie explained.

"Wow! That's slammin'," Brett added. "And you're the producer. The head honcho! Totally cool."

Stephanie smiled. *Darcy, Allie, and Maura were right,* she thought. *It feels good to branch out and make new friends. Everyone in my usual group already knows all this stuff about me. To them it's no big deal. But to Lara, Mark, Caryn, Debbie, June, and Brett, I sound really cool.*

"Do you write the stories for *Scribe TV?*" Brett asked.

Stephanie nodded. "Some of them," she replied.

"Stephanie is an awesome writer," Lara went on. "And she's great in social studies, too."

"It's really nice of you to help Lara out," Debbie said.

"Oh! Are *you* the one who's helping Lara in social studies?" June asked.

Stephanie nodded.

Lara put an arm around Stephanie's shoulders. "When I told Stephanie how far behind I was in Cropple's class, she immediately offered to give me a hand."

"Stephanie Tanner to the rescue!" Mark said with a little grin.

Stephanie's eyes met Mark's green ones.

He held her gaze—a moment longer than he had to, Stephanie thought. Her heart fluttered. "Oh, it's nothing really," she managed to say.

"Hey," Mark suddenly said. "Check it out! They have a Twister stand here." He pointed across the food court to a pretzel stand that looked brand-new.

"Those are the most awesome pretzels in the

world," Mark went on. "I'm going to get one. Anybody else want one?"

Mark collected money from June and Brett. Then he turned to go.

"Hey, Mark!" Lara called. "You're never going to be able to carry all that stuff by yourself. Why don't you take Stephanie with you? She can help."

Stephanie's eyes went wide. Time alone with Mark? Yes! She wanted nothing more than to go with him, but her feet seemed to be frozen to the floor.

She felt a shove from behind. She turned and saw Lara pushing her toward Mark. Lara gave her a look that said "Go!"

"What are you doing?" Stephanie whispered.

"Look, you're helping me out with social studies. I'm helping you out with Mark. It's the least I can do," Lara whispered back. "I can tell that you like him."

Stephanie didn't know how Lara found out about her crush on Mark, but she sure was glad Lara wanted to help them get together.

"Stephanie, are you coming?" Mark called out.

Lara gave her a huge smile. "Now, go!"

"Yeah. Coming, Mark!" she grabbed her mini backpack and grinned at Lara. "See you in a bit," she said. She jogged over to Mark, and the two of them walked to the other end of the food court.

As they passed Pizza Paradise, Stephanie imagined what it would be like to go on a date with Mark. They would make a cute couple, she decided. She was just the perfect height for him.

She tried to imagine how it would feel to hold Mark's strong, callused hand.

"Hey, over this way," Mark told her. He grabbed her hand to guide her toward the pretzel stand.

Stephanie sucked in her breath. His hand was so warm. And it felt so good wrapped around hers.

"They make the best pretzels," Mark explained. "Some of them come dipped in butter and covered with salt. I could eat them all day!"

Stephanie listened as Mark explained all the varieties and flavors to her.

She wished he would go on explaining forever.

"Can I help you?" a boy behind the counter asked.

Mark dropped Stephanie's hand and placed their order. When it came time to carry the pretzels to the group, Stephanie felt a twinge of disappointment. *I love spending time alone with Mark,* she thought. *I wish we didn't have to go back so soon.*

As they walked toward the fountain, Mark told Stephanie about his football practice that afternoon. The guys on his team had all played a joke on their coach by switching the practice ball with one made out of chocolate.

"Really?" Stephanie asked with a laugh. "And he fell for it?"

Mark's face lit up. "Hook, line, and sinker!" he said. "You should have seen his expression when he caught the ball and the chocolate smudged all over his hands!"

Stephanie laughed.

"When he realized what was going on, Coach Ripley *ate* the entire football." Mark chuckled.

"That's the funniest!" Stephanie laughed. "Imagine how he would have looked in the school newspaper if someone got a picture of him with the ball in his mouth!"

Mark stopped walking. "Hey," he said. "You know, a lot of girls just aren't interested when I talk about the team. Lara's right about you—you are pretty special."

Stephanie felt her face grow hot and knew she was blushing. She looked down and pretended to adjust the pretzels she was carrying. "Uh, thanks," she replied.

The two of them stood silently for a moment, gazing at the ground.

"Hey! I've got an idea." Mark broke the silence. "Why don't you come to my game Saturday night. Then afterward, maybe we can go to a movie or something."

Had she heard right? Was Mark Votto, the gorgeous high school quarterback, asking her on a date? "Excuse me?" Stephanie said.

Mark moved a bit closer. "Stephanie, I'm asking you if you'd like to go out with me Saturday night."

Whoa! she thought excitedly. *He* did *ask me out on a date!*

Stephanie wanted to spike the pretzels and do a touchdown dance right there in the food court. *Easy*, she coached herself. *You don't want him to think you're a complete weirdo.* "Great," she said casually. "I mean—Saturday night sounds great."

Mark smiled. "Excellent." They began walking toward the rest of the group again. "Hey, you know what?"

Stephanie shook her head. "No. What?" she asked.

"This may sound mean, but I'm glad Lara is such a lamebrain in social studies," Mark admitted.

"Why?" Stephanie asked, confused.

"If she weren't, I might never have gotten the chance to meet you," he said with a laugh.

Stephanie realized that *she* was happy Lara needed help in social studies, too.

In fact, she had made the deal of a lifetime with Lara. For agreeing to do just a tiny bit of tutoring—she was now dating the cutest guy in all of San Francisco!

CHAPTER
5

Stephanie jumped to her feet and cheered as the adorable Number Twenty-three, Mark Votto, raced downfield, the football tucked snugly under his arm.

He dodged left, avoiding an opposing player. Then he leapt, escaping the diving tackle of another. Stephanie bit her fingernail. Would he make it?

He crossed the twenty-yard line. The fifteen. The ten!

Closer—closer he ran to the end zone, till there was no one around to stop him—

Touchdown!

The crowd exploded into cheers. Mark's team won the high school national championships!

Stephanie cheered louder than anyone.

"Votto! Votto! Votto!" millions of people cried.

Stephanie thought she would explode from sheer happiness. Mark shielded his eyes from the sun and searched the stands. When he finally spotted Stephanie, he pointed at her, then blew her a kiss. Stephanie's heart felt as though it were melting.

"I'm proud of my win," Mark told the dozens of reporters surrounding him. "But I can't take all the credit. Half of this win goes to the most wonderful girl in the world. My smart, beautiful girlfriend, Stephanie Tanner. Stephanie Tanner. Stephanie. Stephanie. Stephanie . . ."

"Stephanie! Stephanie! Come on, wake up!" She felt something tugging on her nightshirt.

She rolled over in her bed. What was going on? Where was Mark? Where were all the reporters?

"Mark?" Stephanie asked sleepily.

"Mark? No, it's me. *Michelle.* Snap out of it! You were dreaming!"

Stephanie frowned, then rubbed her eyes. Slowly she opened them. She stared at her familiar bedroom walls and sighed.

"Wow, I was having *the* most incredible dream," she said with a yawn. Then she hit Michelle with her pillow. "What did you wake me up for?"

"You have to help me!" Michelle exclaimed. "What am I going to do?"

Stephanie sat up instantly. "What's wrong?"

Michelle cringed. "I slept through Flourie's three o'clock feeding," she confessed sadly. "I set my alarm clock, but I must not have heard it."

Stephanie stared intently at her sister. "Okay—then what happened."

Michelle's eyes widened. "Nothing. That's it!" she cried. "I didn't feed Flourie like I was supposed to!"

Stephanie rolled her eyes. *This was the big emergency?* She glanced at her alarm clock. "Michelle, it's only seven A.M.," she pointed out. "Just feed her now and stop bothering me."

Michelle stared back at her sister in disbelief. "Feed her *now?*" she snapped. "But it's four hours too late! I missed it. And I'm supposed to mark down that I missed it on Flourie's chart."

"Michelle, you're making a huge deal out of nothing," Stephanie said.

"But I messed up," Michelle whined. "Mrs. Yoshida will know I messed up. And then I won't get the Best Parent award!"

Stephanie rolled her eyes as she fluffed up her pillow and turned back to her sister.

"Look," she began, "do you see Mrs. Yoshida here in this room?"

Michelle made a face. "No," she replied.

"Right. And was Mrs. Yoshida here, in this room, at three o'clock this morning?" Stephanie asked.

"No," Michelle said quietly.

"Okay, then," Stephanie proclaimed. "Give Flourie her bottle now, and just put a check on the chart!"

Michelle hesitated. "But—I don't know if I'm allowed to do that," she said.

Stephanie stood and pulled on her robe. She picked up a pen and made a big black check on Michelle's flour-baby chart.

"Then *I'll* do it!" she said. She bent down and took Flourie from her cradle—the same cradle Stephanie had used for her baby dolls years before.

"Now give her a bottle. I'm going to take my shower." She tossed the flour sack to Michelle, who let out a shriek.

"Flourie!" Michelle caught Flourie inches before the flour sack hit the floor. "You almost killed her!"

"Michelle! She's just a baking ingredient!" Stephanie pointed out.

"No, she's not. She's my baby!"

Stephanie took a deep breath. "All right. I'm sorry. But trust me, just feed Flourie now and forget about it. Your teacher will never know the difference."

Michelle smiled. "Thanks, Steph."

"No problem," Stephanie answered. She smiled to herself as she made her way toward the bathroom. First she promised to give Lara a hand, and now Michelle. *It feels really good to help people when they need you,* she thought.

If only Michelle hadn't woken her up during the best part of her dream. The part where Mark might have kissed her!

When she reached school that morning, Stephanie rushed to the pay phone next to the cafeteria. Darcy, Allie, and Maura were all waiting for her.

"So?" Darcy asked when Stephanie reached them. "How did it go at the mall last night?"

"Yeah," Maura chimed in. "Spill everything. I want details."

Stephanie smiled mysteriously. "We just hung out at the mall. What else is there to say?"

"I know that smile, Stephanie." Allie gazed piercingly into her eyes. "There's more than that. I know it. Now, talk."

"There's really nothing else," Stephanie teased. "Oh! Except for the fact that Mark Votto asked me out on a date."

"What?" Darcy squealed. "That is so totally awesome! You've got a date with one of the guys from high school. A football player. And not just a football player, the quarterback!"

"The good part is, Lara made it all possible. She told Mark what a great person I am. She even arranged for the two of us to be alone," Stephanie told her friends. "You guys were totally wrong about her. She's completely nice."

"Wow, Steph. We're really happy for you," Maura admitted. "I'm glad we were wrong about Lara."

"Yeah, especially since now you can invite us to the mall with your new friends," Darcy said. "Then a high school crowd, and football players—and *romance*—will be around the corner for all four of us!"

Stephanie laughed. "I think you're getting a little carried away," she told her friend.

"No. Seriously, Steph, don't mess up this thing with Lara and Mark. It's our big chance to be with the coolest crowd ever. And chances like this come only once. It's all up to you!"

Stephanie sat cross-legged on the grass in front of her school, along with the rest of her social studies class. The bright sun beat down, warming her face.

Lara plopped down beside her. "This is *sooo* great!" she chirped.

"Having class outside is the best idea ever! Ms. Cropple is awesome!" Stephanie agreed.

"So," Lara whispered, "we're still getting together for the take-home tonight, aren't we?"

Stephanie nodded. Everyone knew Ms. Cropple was giving a take-home quiz at the end of class. Stephanie still felt a bit guilty about working with Lara on it. Especially since Ms. Cropple made it clear that every student should work on the quiz alone.

But think about it, she reasoned to herself. *Lara's been such a good friend these past few days. She's even helping to get me together with Mark. Giving her a hand on one little take-home quiz is the least I can do for her.*

"Yes, we're on," Stephanie whispered back. "Why don't you come over to my house after dinner, at about six-thirty?"

"Great!" Lara smiled. "So—do you know the stuff? Because I'm, like, not quite ready."

Stephanie stared at her. *Of course* she knew the material. They'd only been learning it every day this past week.

"Yeah, I know it," she whispered back.

A strange feeling began forming in Stephanie's stomach. What did Lara mean when she said she "wasn't quite ready" for the quiz?

CHAPTER
6

◆ ◀ ◢ ◆

"Now, come on, little Flourie," Danny Tanner cooed. "Time for dinner. Open up for Grandpa. I have some delicious strained carrots for you to eat. Yummy, yummy!"

"Grandpa?" Stephanie's older sister, D.J., asked. She leaned over toward Stephanie. "Dad's taking this a bit seriously, isn't he?"

Stephanie nodded. "He sure is." She stared at her father with a slight smile on her face. It was all she could do to keep from laughing. She knew Danny liked to help with homework projects, but this was ridiculous. Her father was pretending to feed baby food to a sack of flour!

Not only that, Flourie was seated at the dinner

table with the rest of her family. Michelle had taken one of Alex's old high chairs and sat Flourie in it at the head of the table.

Even more ridiculous—Flourie was now wearing a pink baby bonnet!

"Dad," Stephanie joked, "should I get the baking powder out of the cabinet so you can take care of it next?"

Danny frowned. "Come on, Stephanie. We're all trying to help Michelle here."

He turned back to Flourie. Then, in his best talking-to-a-baby voice, he said, "What's the matter, Flourie? You don't *like* strained carrots?"

Stephanie poked Joey Gladstone, who was sitting next to her. "Maybe it reminds her of a carrot cake she once knew," she whispered.

Joey cracked up, nearly spitting his water out onto the kitchen table.

"I knew I could count on *you* to appreciate my humor," she told him. Joey was totally funny. That's how he and Danny became friends, by telling jokes together.

Then, when Stephanie's mother died in a car accident, Joey came to live with the Tanners.

"Your father seems very proud of his *grandflour*," Joey whispered back.

Stephanie giggled. Good thing *Joey* had a sense of humor about this whole thing.

Stephanie watched as Danny tied a bib around Flourie. "We don't want a messy-wessy now, do we?"

Stephanie's eyes widened. *Messy-wessy?* Her father was losing his *mind!*

Danny caught Stephanie's gaze. "Okay," he admitted, "maybe that was a little much."

Michelle strolled into the kitchen. "Here, honey," Danny said. "Put this plastic mat down around Flourie's high chair. Babies can be very messy eaters," Danny instructed.

Michelle smiled. *"Tell* me about it, Dad. Flourie is about the messiest baby around."

"Look, Flourie!" Stephanie's uncle Jesse cried. He covered his eyes with his hands, then pulled them away. "Peek-a-boo!"

Stephanie shook her head. "Oh, no! Not you, too!"

Uncle Jesse had also moved in with Stephanie and her family after her mother died. A few years later he married Becky. Soon after, Jesse and Becky had twin boys—her cousins Nicky and Alex. Now they all lived in the attic apartment upstairs.

"Stephanie, we're *all* trying to help Michelle with her project," Danny said sternly. "This is for school, and she really wants to get a good grade. So I think it would be nice if you helped out, too. If you can't do that, I'd appreciate it if you would just stay out of it."

Stephanie frowned. She put some linguini onto her dinner plate and settled back in her chair. "You're right. Sorry." She twisted a forkful of linguini, then took a bite.

"Hey, I wonder if Flourie can eat linguini?" she whispered to Joey.

Joey chuckled. "I don't know," he whispered back. "That pasta could have been made with a relative or something."

Stephanie giggled. Danny shot both her and Joey a disapproving look.

"You know, Michelle," Danny said loudly, "I think Joey and your big sister Stephanie would like to help you, too. Maybe each of them can baby-sit for Flourie one night this week?"

Stephanie's eyes widened. What if Danny just volunteered her to flour-sit on the night of her date with Mark? *"Dad,"* she said through her clenched teeth.

"Really?" Michelle asked. "Can you?"

Stephanie stared at her father. She realized he wasn't going to give her any choice. She could only pray Michelle wouldn't need her on Saturday night.

She sighed. "Yeah, sure," she said. "I'll flour-sit—I mean, baby-sit for Flourie."

Stephanie finished her dinner and helped clear the table. Just as she was finishing, the front doorbell rang.

Stephanie ran to get it, and found Lara standing on her front step.

Stephanie introduced Lara to her family. Then the two of them headed upstairs to Stephanie's room.

"Where was this taken?" Lara asked, picking up a photograph from Stephanie's desk.

"That's my family at Uncle Jesse and Aunt Becky's wedding," Stephanie told her.

"And what's this?" Lara wondered.

"It's my first front-page article in *The Scribe*," Stephanie explained. "My dad had it framed for me."

"You share a room with your sister?" Lara asked, pointing to Michelle's bed.

Stephanie nodded.

"Me, too," Lara said with a sigh. "It's the absolute worst!"

Stephanie was glad to have another thing in common with her new friend.

"Michelle isn't so bad," Stephanie admitted. "Usually we get along pretty well."

"What's all this?" Lara asked. She was pointing to Flourie's wall chart.

"Don't ask," Stephanie replied. "It's part of a

51

project Michelle is doing for school. And speaking of school, we should really get to work. We've got a lot of material to cover for this test."

Lara smiled. "Yeah, okay. Down to business." She pulled the chair from Michelle's desk over to Stephanie's desk. Then she sat down and opened her bookbag. She placed her notebook and take-home quiz on her lap.

"Okay, question one," Stephanie started in. " 'Who was the Shoshone girl who helped famous explorers Lewis and Clark on their northwestern expedition?' " She paused. "Easy! We should have this in our notes from last week, actually."

Stephanie flipped through the few pages of notes she had taken from class that day. She thought she knew the answer but wanted to make sure she was right. Yup. There it was: Sacajawea. She wrote the name down on her test.

Stephanie glanced up at Lara. She was frantically flipping through her notebook, a worried expression fixed on her face. After a few minutes she looked up. "Uh—is it Pocahontas?"

"*Pocahontas?*" Stephanie exclaimed. "She died way before the Lewis and Clark expedition!"

Lara slammed her notebook down in disgust. "Oh, Stephanie. It's hopeless!" she exclaimed. "My notes are awful. Just look at them."

Stephanie took Lara's notebook. She opened it and gasped. It was a jumbled mess inside. Doodles, love notes, and song lyrics filled most of the pages. There were a few class notes woven into the mess, but nothing of any substance.

"I goofed off most of the semester," Lara admitted. "Until I realized that I *had* to do well in this class. I'm going to do better from now on—really—but I just need to get through this test.

"Please, Stephanie," she begged. "Please help me get through this!"

Stephanie couldn't believe it. Lara wanted Stephanie to give her the answers to the quiz!

I can't do it, Stephanie told herself. *I just can't.*

"Um, Lara," she started to say. Then she glanced at Lara's face. She appeared frantic, worried.

In a word, Stephanie thought, *pathetic.*

Lara does *want my answers, but it isn't because she's being manipulating or mean, like Allie and Maura thought*, Stephanie realized. *She wants them because she's in trouble.*

Can I really say no to her? Stephanie wondered. *Can I tell my new friend that I won't help her out of a tight spot?*

Stephanie closed her eyes. She needed to figure out what to do. But all she could think of was Mark Votto. Her big movie date with him was only two days away.

And it's thanks to Lara that you're even going! she reminded herself. How could she not help Lara when Lara was doing so much to help *her?*

"Please, Stephanie?" Lara asked again. "I really need your help."

Stephanie took a deep breath and made her decision.

"The answer is—Sacajawea," she replied quietly.

CHAPTER
7

Stephanie sipped her soda, then lifted a french fry off her plate. She reached for the little paper cup of ketchup sitting in front of her. But instead of dipping her fry, she bumped hands with Mark. He was trying to dip his fry at the same time.

"I'll fight you for it!" Mark joked. "We can have a french fry sword fight to see who gets the ketchup."

Stephanie giggled. "Okay, *en garde!*" They fought until Mark's french fry broke hers in half.

"No fair," Stephanie cried. "You didn't tell me you were fighting with an extra crispy fry."

"Ha!" Mark cried. "All is fair in love and food.

Now, I will take your weapon!" He plucked the other half of Stephanie's broken fry out of the ketchup and shoved it in his mouth.

Stephanie laughed out loud. She couldn't believe how much fun she was having with Mark. The Jim Carrey movie they had just seen was hysterical! And now they were laughing together over their shared order of fries at Burger Buddy.

Stephanie decided this was the best date she'd ever been on.

The coolest part, of course, was being seen with Mark, the sweet, handsome, funny high-school football player. She made sure to wave to everyone she knew from school.

"So, did you like the movie?" she asked.

"It was great," Mark said. "Jim Carrey is my idol . . . he's such a riot."

Stephanie agreed. Jim Carrey cracked her up, too.

"I'm glad that Lara introduced us," Mark added. "I'm having a good time with you."

Stephanie felt her face redden. *I was just thinking the same thing.*

"You know, you're just so—sweet!" Mark exclaimed. "Lara told me how much you helped her in social studies."

Mark leaned in close. Stephanie couldn't help but notice how incredibly green his eyes were.

And how they sparkled when the light hit them just right.

"You offered to help her," Mark continued, "without even knowing how important it is for the cheerleading squad."

Stephanie paused. "Wait—helping Lara in Ms. Cropple's class is good for the cheerleaders?" she asked, confused. "How?"

"Well, the cheerleaders just made it to the all-state championship cheer competition," Mark explained.

"And what does this have to do with me?" Stephanie wondered.

Mark smirked. "I'm getting to that, Ms. Investigative Reporter." He paused to take a sip of soda. "The high school has a policy. If you're failing any of your classes, you're not allowed to be in any extracurricular activities."

"And . . ." Stephanie led him on.

"*And* Lara is failing Ms. Cropple's class," Mark finished.

"*Failing?*" Stephanie said. "She told me she was way behind—not *failing!*"

Mark shrugged. "Maybe she was embarrassed to admit it to you."

Stephanie thought that made sense. If she were failing, *she* wouldn't want to admit it, either.

"Anyway," Mark continued, "she's failed

every one of Ms. Cropple's tests and quizzes, so there's a good chance she'll fail the term.

"She's on academic warning right now," Mark went on. "If she gets an F in Ms. Cropple's class this term—she'll be kicked off the cheerleading squad. And the squad will never win the all-state championship without Lara."

"Whoa." It was all Stephanie could think to say.

Stephanie lifted her glass of soda and sat back in her seat. As she sipped, she thought about Lara's predicament. She felt bad for her new friend. Cheerleading was her life. Just like *The Scribe* and *Scribe TV* were Stephanie's life.

Stephanie knew she'd be *totally* miserable if she ever got kicked out of those activities.

"All the girls in our group will be totally crushed if they don't win at states. Plus, a lot of my buddies on the football team date the cheerleaders! *They* want their girlfriends to win, too.

"The way we see it," Mark concluded, "if you can help Lara get better grades, she'll be able to stay on the squad. And that will be awesome news for the cheerleaders. And everyone in my group. And the whole high school." He chuckled. "In fact, you'd practically be a national hero if Lara passes the term."

Oh, great! Stephanie thought. *The fate of the entire high school rests on my shoulders!* She sighed.

"Well, I can try to help Lara," she said. "But I'm not a magician or anything. She has to do well on the next two tests—on her own—to get a passing grade and stay on the squad. There are no more take-home quizzes this term."

Mark smiled at her. "I'm sure she can do it . . . with your help."

"I sure hope so," Stephanie said.

Stephanie raced right to the telephone after Mark dropped her off at home. *It's not too late to call the girls and give them an update,* she thought.

Once she got Allie on the line, Allie called Darcy on her three-way calling. Then Stephanie dialed Maura's number on the fax phone in her father's home office. She connected the extensions so they could all speak.

"Guys, it was the most incredible, unbelievable, wonderful, awesome, excellent, terrific date ever!" Stephanie gushed.

"So things didn't go very well with Mark, huh?" Darcy joked.

Everyone laughed.

"Tell us everything!" Allie pleaded.

"Yeah," Maura chimed in. "Like, for instance,

how you got your father to let you go on a date with a high school guy."

"Actually, Dad was pretty cool about the whole thing," Stephanie told them. "He did have to meet Mark, and ask him where we were going. But he said if Mark's mother drove us both ways, and I was home by ten, I could go."

"The date," Maura reminded her. "Tell us about your date."

Stephanie smiled. "Well, we went to the Jim Carrey movie and then to Burger Buddy," Stephanie told them.

"*And?*" Darcy prodded.

"The movie was so funny," Stephanie said. "Mark thought so, too. We have the same sense of humor," she added. "We laughed at all the same parts, and there was this one part we both thought was totally stupid."

"No one cares about the plot of the movie. Did you hold hands?" Allie wanted to know.

"Not during the movie," Stephanie admitted. "But a little at Burger Buddy."

"Did he kiss you?" Darcy asked.

"No," Stephanie replied. "There wasn't really a good time to kiss. We left the movie, then Burger Buddy was so crowded. And then his mother came to get us, and she was watching us the whole time."

"Did he ask you out again?" Darcy asked.

"Well, sort of," Stephanie replied. "I mean, it's not definite."

"Hey, does Mark have a cute friend? You can set me up," Darcy suggested. "Maybe we can double or something."

Stephanie laughed. "This was a *date*, Darcy. His friends weren't hanging out with us tonight."

"So when are you going to get us in with your new, older crowd?" Darcy demanded.

"If things keep going this well with Mark, pretty soon we'll all be hanging out with Mark and Lara and their friends!" Stephanie announced.

"Cool. Oh! I never asked, how did your studying with Lara go?" Darcy asked.

Stephanie stopped. She wanted to let her friends know that things hadn't gone all that well. She wanted to tell them how she gave Lara the answers to the take-home quiz—and how guilty she felt about it.

But she couldn't. She knew Allie and Maura would think Lara was up to no good—just as they had when Lara first asked for help.

But Stephanie had been there when Lara freaked out about her notes. She understood how important cheerleading was to Lara. Maura and Allie would never see that side of it. They'd never understand that Stephanie *had* to help Lara.

"Things went great with Lara," Stephanie reported. "In fact, I'm sure she did extremely well on the take-home quiz."

Extremely well, she thought. *She used my answers. I just hope no one ever finds out about it.*

CHAPTER
8

Monday morning Stephanie pushed herself away from Ms. Cropple's desk. She stretched and yawned. Her neck muscles ached from looking down at her work for so long.

Whoa! I didn't realize that grading homework assignments could be such a pain in the neck! Stephanie thought. She chuckled to herself.

A soft tapping came from the door. Stephanie glanced up. *That's weird*, Stephanie thought. *I'm supposed to be alone in the resource center this period. All the teachers are in class.*

She opened the door to find Lara standing in the hall with a huge grin. "Hey! I thought you'd be here! Ms. Cropple stopped me in the hall this morning," she said. "She told me I did great on the take-home quiz!"

Stephanie smiled. That meant *her* grade must have been high, too. After all, their answers were identical.

Then Stephanie stopped. The idea of the two of them having the same answers gave her a guilty pang inside. *Maybe I should tell her*, Stephanie thought. *Maybe I should mention how uncomfortable I feel about sharing answers—and tell her I never want to do it again. After all, if we're friends, I should be able to tell Lara anything, right?*

"That's really great, Lara," she said. "That grade will definitely bring your overall average up. But there's something I have to tell you."

"No, wait," Lara interrupted. "There's something I have to tell you first." She peered into the resource room. "Can I come in?"

Stephanie hesitated. Students weren't supposed to be in the room when no teachers were around. Not without special permission.

But it's only Lara, Stephanie reasoned. *I can trust her. It will be fine for just a few minutes or so.*

Stephanie opened the door wider. "Okay, come on in. But just for a little while."

Lara stepped through the doorway. "Here's the thing, Steph," she started. "I know you didn't feel comfortable giving me those quiz answers. And I want you to know, I felt uncomfortable, too. Let's not ever do that again, okay? When we study together, we'll *work* together. Okay?"

Whew! Stephanie thought. *I didn't have to say anything. Lara knew just how I was feeling. She is a good friend!*

"Okay," Stephanie agreed. "We'll work together."

Lara glanced at the papers Stephanie was grading. "Want some help?" she asked. "If I help, you'll finish in half the time."

Stephanie split the pile of papers in half and pushed one half to Lara. "Here's the answer key," she said.

The two of them started in on their stacks. They had gotten about halfway through, when another knock sounded on the door. Stephanie turned to see Mark peeking at her through the tiny door window.

She turned to Lara. "It's Mark!" she whispered.

Lara smiled knowingly. "I told him you might be here this period."

Stephanie grinned. Lara had told Mark where to find her! Awesome!

She opened the door. "Hi!" she said cheerfully.

Mark smiled, displaying that perfect set of dimples Stephanie had been dreaming about all night.

"Hi! Can you come out in the hall for a sec?" he asked.

Stephanie giggled. As if she would actually say no.

"I'll be right back!" she whispered to Lara.

"No problem. I've got enough to keep me busy here," Lara responded.

Stephanie stepped into the empty hallway and closed the door behind her—just so they could have a little privacy. Lara didn't have to know *everything* about her relationship with Mark.

"I wanted to tell you—I had a lot of fun Saturday night," Mark said.

"Me, too," Stephanie replied. "A lot."

"Great! Then let's do it again. Maybe this weekend?" Mark asked.

Stephanie nodded eagerly. *Yes!* she thought. Ever since Mark's mother dropped her off at home, she'd been hoping Mark would ask her on another date. "I would love to," she said.

Mark's face lit up. "Great!" he said. "Wherever you want to go. A movie, skating, whatever."

Stephanie's heart skipped a beat. Mark definitely had the promise of being the world's most incredible boyfriend.

"Stephanie." Mark leaned in close, his voice suddenly soft. "Is it okay . . . I mean, do you mind if I . . . well, can I kiss you?"

Stephanie wasn't sure she'd heard him correctly. But before she could say "What?" Mark kissed her. Right there in the hallway.

Stephanie felt dizzy. She couldn't believe what had just happened. Mark kissed her!

And it was the most perfect kiss ever.

Mark stared into Stephanie's eyes. Then he glanced at the clock in the hall.

"Whoa! I need to get back to the high school and my locker, and fast!" He squeezed Stephanie's hand. "So, I'll see you later, okay?"

Stephanie nodded her reply. Mark's kiss had left her speechless.

She watched as he ran down the hall. Before he disappeared from sight, he turned and gave Stephanie a wave. She waved back, then stepped inside the resource room. She pulled the door closed and leaned against it.

She couldn't help smiling the biggest, silliest smile ever. She reached up to touch her lips right where Mark had kissed her.

"What's up?" Lara asked. "You look . . . I don't know, goofy."

"You won't believe this!" Stephanie gushed to Lara. "Promise not to tell anyone?"

Lara nodded eagerly. "Yes, I promise. What is it?"

"Mark just kissed me!" Stephanie exclaimed.

Lara's eyes widened, and she grinned from ear to ear. "Stephanie! That's excellent! I knew you and Mark would make a great couple."

Stephanie fell into her chair and spun around happily. This was the best day she'd ever had. It was a day she was going to have to put in her diary and celebrate every year from then on.

"So, Stephanie," Lara said. "I'm late already. I have to get back to the high school for my algebra class. Are we on for tonight, or what?"

"Tonight?" Stephanie asked.

"Yes, tonight!" Lara reminded her. "We have a major test tomorrow! I thought we were going to study together!"

"Right! The test!" Stephanie remembered. "Sure, we're studying together. Why don't you come over to my house after dinner tonight?"

Lara gave Stephanie a huge hug. "You're the best!" she exclaimed. "And I'm really happy for you and Mark."

Lara left the room and Stephanie touched her lips again. *Happy* didn't even come close to describing the way she was feeling right then.

Totally and completely ecstatic!
Now, that was more like it!

The phone rang as Stephanie was clearing the last dirty plate from the kitchen table. She ran to the living room to get it.

"Hello?" she answered.

"Stephanie? It's Darcy."

"Oh, hi. What's up?" Stephanie flopped down on the couch.

"Well, Allie and Maura are here. We're wondering if you want to come over and study with us tonight," Darcy asked.

"I can't," Stephanie told her. "I told Lara I'd study with her for the social studies test tonight."

"Hey! Why don't you bring Lara to my house, too?" Darcy suggested. "That way we'll all get to meet her. And we'll all be one step closer to being in her super cool group."

"Darce, it's really important that I get Lara through these next few tests. Then I'll talk to her about hanging out with you guys. Really," Stephanie promised.

"Give her a break, Darcy!" Stephanie could hear Allie in the background.

"Listen," Darcy continued. "I'm counting on you, Stephanie. I'm totally in love with that running back you pointed out—Brett Johnson. The only way we'll ever get together is if I start hanging out with Lara and her group. So make sure she does well on those tests—and slip in a couple of mentions about your other friends. Okay?"

Stephanie sighed. As if Mark hadn't put enough pressure on her to make sure Lara did well, now Darcy was doing it to her, too!

"Sure, Darcy. I'll do my best," Stephanie promised. She hung up the phone and climbed the stairs to her room. Michelle was standing by her bed, trying to perch Flourie on her shoulder.

Stephanie frowned. "What are you doing?"

"I'm trying to figure out how to burp Flourie," Michelle answered. "But I don't think I'm doing it right."

"That's because you're *not* doing it right," Stephanie said. "You're not supposed to put the *whole* baby on your shoulder. Here, let me show you." She took Flourie from Michelle.

"Lean her—er—body against your chest and put only her head above your shoulder. Then, rub her back with gentle circular motions." Stephanie demonstrated. She had done this a hundred times with Nicky and Alex.

Stephanie looked up when the door to her bedroom opened and Lara strode inside.

"Uh, hi!" she said. "Your father told me I could come on up." She stopped. "What in the world are you doing?"

Stephanie laughed uneasily. "If I told you," she said, "you wouldn't believe me." She turned to Michelle. "Take Flourie downstairs, okay?" she asked. "Lara and I have work to do."

Michelle carefully lifted Flourie from Stephanie's lap. She cradled the flour sack in her arms and headed for the door.

When Michelle was gone, Lara pulled a chair over to Stephanie's desk and took out her books. "So, am I losing my mind, or were you just burping a flour sack?"

Stephanie's face reddened. "It's a project for my sister's class at school. She has to take care of a flour sack as if it were a real baby. I was just helping her . . . well . . . I was helping her burp it, okay?"

"Hey," Lara said. "No problem. But if you're free next weekend, I have a pound of sugar that needs changing."

"Very funny!" Stephanie said. She and Lara both cracked up.

Stephanie was still laughing when Lara opened her bookbag. She pulled out some papers and put them on Stephanie's desk. They were stapled together and were typed.

Could Lara have gone from total mess to Ms. Organized in one week? Stephanie wondered.

"What is that?" she asked. "Did you type up your notes?"

Lara grinned mysteriously. Then she thrust the paper closer for Stephanie to see.

Stephanie stared at the top sheet. Her eyes grew wide. She couldn't believe what she was looking at—a social studies test on Native Americans! She glanced at the name at the top of the test. It was Ms. Cropple's!

"Lara!" Stephanie exclaimed. "This is one of Ms. Cropple's tests!"

Lara nodded.

"But how? When? Where did you get it from?"

Lara folded her arms across her chest and leaned back in her chair. "Relax, Stephanie," she said calmly. "My cousin had Cropple for social studies three years ago, and she saved all the tests. We can use them to study from. Isn't it great that she kept them for me?"

Stephanie kept staring at the paper. The questions might have been from three years ago, but they seemed to cover all the stuff they'd been learning in class for the past month.

"I can't believe your cousin saved this," she said. "It has—*everything* on it."

"Yeah, but it doesn't have the answers," Lara pointed out. "See? We can study from it by looking up all the answers. If we're lucky, maybe the same kinds of questions will be on the test tomorrow."

"I don't know, Lara," Stephanie hesitated. "Isn't this sort of . . . cheating?"

Lara laughed. "No way!" she exclaimed. "We don't have any of the answers," she pointed out. "Plus, we don't even know if these questions will be on our test."

"True," Stephanie said.

"Look, I think that by studying from this old test, we'll be able to narrow down which chapters Cropple might think are the most important. Then we can concentrate on reading those first tonight."

"I guess you're right," she said. "It wouldn't be like Ms. Cropple to use the exact same test over, so, really, it's *not* cheating."

"Right. Now, let's look at question number one. I'll read it out loud." Lara cleared her throat. "Connecticut is home to which tiny Native American nation?"

Stephanie stared blankly. "I have no idea," she said. "It's so hard remembering all those Native American tribe names!"

"Tell me about it," Lara said. "So, let's look it

up. See? We're working here. We're studying! There's no cheating going on at all!"

Stephanie nodded as she flipped through her notes. Lara had a point. She would be reading through these notes anyway. Only now her reading had more of a focus.

Stephanie flipped through her notebook until she found her list of U.S. states and Indian tribes and nations.

"Okay, let's see. The Native Americans from Connecticut are the Mashantucket Pequot. That's going to be hard to remember."

Lara agreed. "Too bad it's not an open-book test," she commented. "Okay. Next question. 'Who was the Shawnee leader who was killed in the War of 1812?' " She wrinkled her brow at Stephanie. "How are we supposed to know that?"

Stephanie laughed. "We *learned* it," she said. "And I think I know it. But let's find the answer in our notes anyway."

Lara flipped through her textbook and found the answer before Stephanie. "It's Tecumseh!" she said happily. She scribbled the answer in her notebook.

Stephanie smiled. Lara seemed really dedicated to working on this practice test. And she was true to her word. She didn't expect Stephanie to give her all the answers. She was really doing her share. Stephanie wrote down the answer. "Okay, what's number three?"

Lara read from the exam. "This one is an essay question. Describe the Shawnee ritual football game." She laughed out loud. "Maybe we need Mark for this question."

Stephanie laughed, too. "I have to admit," she said. "This is a great way to study. I sure am glad your cousin kept her test papers!"

"Me, too," Lara agreed. "Totally glad."

"And the last answer is—Sacajawea," Lara pronounced.

Stephanie closed her notebook and stretched. She glanced at her clock. Nine-thirty. They had been working for hours.

"Whew! Those questions were *tough!*" Stephanie commented.

"Very tough," Lara agreed. She looked at her watch. "And it's later than I thought. My mom will be here any minute. I'd better get ready."

"I'm glad we don't actually have to take *this* test," Stephanie said. "It was awful. And we still have so much reading to do."

A horn sounded outside. Lara gathered her papers and books. "That's my mom." She looked at Stephanie. "Thanks, Steph. I really appreciate your helping me—again."

"No problem," Stephanie assured her as the two headed down the stairs and toward the front door. "You helped me, too, by suggesting we use the old test as a study guide—so consider us even."

Lara smiled. "Okay—even."

"Just go home and read those last three chapters," Stephanie added. "You'll do fine."

"Fine?" Lara said as she stepped toward her mother's car. "I think we're both going to do better than fine on this test. We're going to *ace* it!"

When Lara was gone, Stephanie settled into bed with her social studies book. She wanted to read over the three chapters Ms. Cropple's test focused most on.

She read for a while, then stopped for a moment to rest her eyes. She was shocked to see Michelle already fast asleep across the room! She'd been so involved in studying, she hadn't even noticed her sister getting into bed.

Stephanie headed for the bathroom. When she reached the doorway, she glanced at Flourie's chart. Then she looked at her clock. It was almost eleven o'clock. Flourie was scheduled for a diaper change. Michelle must have forgotten. And now she was fast asleep.

Stephanie sighed deeply. *The last thing I need is for Michelle to freak out the way she did the other morning when she missed Flourie's three A.M. feeding,* Stephanie thought.

Stephanie checked Flourie's chart under "10 P.M. DIAPERED." She pulled a diaper out of the package, crumpled it up, and threw it in the garbage. Michelle would never know she hadn't actually changed the diaper.

There, she thought to herself as she headed for the bathroom. *Michelle gets to be a proud parent— and I get a good night's sleep.*

CHAPTER
9

Stephanie rubbed her tired eyes. *Man,* she thought. *I am* so *beat from studying last night.*

She glanced at the clock. She was a few minutes early for Ms. Cropple's class, but she always liked to be settled in and comfortable before she took a test.

Stephanie turned toward the classroom door just as Lara strolled in looking wide-eyed and rested.

"Good luck, Steph," Lara whispered as she rushed past Stephanie's chair to her own two rows back.

Stephanie smiled and gave her the thumbs-up sign. Ms. Cropple entered and immediately began handing out the exams. Stephanie pulled a pen from her backpack and gazed down at her exam paper.

"Name," she read at the top of the paper. *That's always the easy part!* she joked to herself. She wrote "Stephanie Tanner" in the space provided, then "Social Studies, Period 2, Ms. Cropple" underneath.

So far so good! she thought.

At first glance Stephanie saw the test was a few pages long. She hoped it wasn't too long. Sometimes, even if she knew the material backward and forward, her thoughts became jumbled during long tests.

Question number one, she read to herself. *Connecticut is home to which tiny Native American nation?*

Stephanie smiled. She knew that one! Mashantucket Pequot, she scribbled into the space provided. In fact, a question like that had been on the old test she and Lara had studied from. What good luck!

Question number two. Who was the Shawnee leader who was killed in the War of 1812?

Stephanie stared at the question. *Hey, that question was on the old test, too!*

A strange feeling crept over her as she wrote Tecumseh in the answer space.

Question number three. Describe the Shawnee ritual football game.

Stephanie's mouth fell open. That was on the old test, too. She remembered joking with Lara that Mark would be the best person to answer the question!

Quickly she skimmed through the remaining questions on the test. Her heart began to pound as she read.

Stephanie swallowed hard.

These are the exact same questions that were on the old test last night! she thought in confusion.

And in the exact same order!

A feeling of dread swept over Stephanie as she realized the horrible truth. *This is the exact same test Lara brought over last night!* What was going on?

Stephanie spun around in her seat. She tried to catch Lara's attention, but she was bent over her test paper, writing away happily.

Stephanie gazed around the room. Everyone was deep into their tests.

What should I do? she wondered. *Should I tell Ms. Cropple I've already seen the test and I know all the answers?*

No way, she decided. She didn't think she could stand up in the middle of class and say that.

Stephanie took a deep breath. *There's only one thing I can do,* she thought. She picked up her pen and started writing down the answers to the questions. She filled in every single answer she'd looked up the previous night with Lara.

It wasn't long before she was done with the entire test.

Stephanie gazed up at the clock. There was still half an hour left for the exam! She gulped. What in the world was she going to do for another thirty minutes?

To kill time, Stephanie retraced her answers with her pen. When she was done, she glanced over at the clock again.

Oh, great! she thought. *That took a whole ten minutes! Now what?*

Just then, Stephanie heard Ms. Cropple's chair scrape against the floor.

She watched in horror as her teacher got up from her desk and began to walk around the room.

Ms. Cropple stopped at all the students' desks and checked to see how they were doing.

Stephanie began to panic. *What if Ms. Cropple sees my paper?* she thought worriedly. *What if she sees that I'm finished already?*

Stephanie leaned over her paper and pretended to write. She heard Ms. Cropple walking closer and closer.

Stephanie picked up her exam and pretended to reread a question on the first page. She frowned deeply, trying to make it seem as if she were concentrating—and couldn't be disturbed.

But Ms. Cropple stopped directly in front of her desk.

Stephanie sat frozen in horror. Ms. Cropple was sure to ask how she had finished her test in just twenty minutes.

And Stephanie knew she had no answer.

"Stephanie," Ms. Cropple said.

Stephanie gulped. This was it. She was caught. She looked up at her teacher.

"Can you help me out during fifth period today?" Ms. Cropple asked. "I need some homework assignments graded."

Homework assignments? Stephanie breathed a huge sigh of relief. Ms. Cropple hadn't even noticed she was finished! She placed her exam facedown on her desk and nodded.

"Great," Ms. Cropple told her. "I'll see you then." She quietly strolled to the next student's desk.

Stephanie slumped in her chair. *That was close!* she thought nervously.

For the next twenty minutes, Stephanie prayed

Ms. Cropple wouldn't get up again. Luckily, her teacher spent the rest of the time at her desk. When there were only five minutes left before the bell, Stephanie's classmates began handing in their papers.

She watched their faces as they left the room. It was obvious her classmates found the test very difficult.

Stephanie decided to wait to hand in her exam. She wanted to hand hers in with Lara's, so the two could talk on the way out of class.

She and Lara had to figure out what to do about seeing the test ahead of time. She *had* to find out from Lara what she thought they should do.

Stephanie was sure they needed to tell Ms. Cropple they'd had the old test to study from. After all, it was the only fair thing they could do.

She watched as Lara wrote, noting that her friend was really good at dragging out taking the test. Finally Lara put down her pen. She picked up her bookbag and her exam and walked across the room to hand it to Ms. Cropple.

"How did it go, Lara?" Ms. Cropple asked.

Stephanie watched as Lara pretended to breathe a sigh of relief. Then Lara smiled. "Wow,

Ms. Cropple. That was tough! I sure hope I did okay!"

Stephanie listened in shock. *Why is Lara acting as if she didn't do well?* she wondered. *We had all the answers! She's going to get an A plus!*

Lara grinned at Stephanie, then headed for the door. Stephanie quickly handed in her exam and followed Lara out into the hallway.

When Stephanie reached the door, Lara was already down the hall, heading back to the high school for her next class.

"Wait up!" Stephanie called out. She caught up to Lara. "What was that all about?" she asked.

Lara frowned. "What do you mean?"

"I *mean,* what was the deal with that test? We had all the answers! How did that happen? And an even better question—what are we going to do about it?"

Lara stared at Stephanie in confusion. "What are you talking about, Stephanie?"

Stephanie gazed at Lara in shock. Didn't she *realize* that the test was the exact same one they had seen the night before?

"Lara!" Stephanie whispered. "We have to do something about this."

Lara laughed. "Sure we do. Personally, *I'm*

going to celebrate. I'm finally digging myself out of this social studies mess."

Stephanie's eyes narrowed. The halls were filling up with kids, and she didn't want anyone to hear them. "We have to tell Ms. Cropple we had the old test last night!" she said in a low voice. "It's not fair that we knew the questions beforehand. We had all night to look up the answers. No one else had that advantage!" She paused. "Face it—we *cheated!*"

"Listen, Stephanie," Lara snapped. "I don't know what you're getting so hysterical about, but I have to get to my next class. Can we talk about this later, please?"

"When?" Stephanie demanded. Waiting to discuss this would only make her more upset.

"*Later,*" Lara emphasized. Then she disappeared in a crowd of kids.

In shock, Stephanie watched her leave. She couldn't believe Lara was taking this whole thing so lightly. Didn't she understand what they had done? They had the answers to an exam the night *before* the exam.

Stephanie gulped.

Wait, she thought nervously. *Maybe I haven't really cheated. So, I knew all the answers ahead of time. But I still had to do all the work to get the*

answers. And I didn't know *I was cheating. Don't
you have to cheat deliberately for it to really count?*

That thought made her feel a tiny bit better—
but not for long.

At lunchtime Stephanie found Darcy, Allie,
and Maura at their usual table in the middle-
school cafeteria.

Steph sat down next to her friends.

She opened her lunch and glanced around the
table. Allie and Maura were frowning. "Look,
guys," Stephanie started. "I know we haven't
been hanging out very much lately. But that's
going to change. I promise."

"That's not why we're upset," Allie admitted.

"Oh. Then, why are you upset?" Stephanie asked.

"Ms. Cropple's test." Darcy moaned. "It was
so hard! I couldn't believe those questions!"

"I must have changed my answers at least ten
times!" Allie agreed.

"And what about all those tribe names?"
Maura asked. "I wish I'd known Ms. Cropple
expected us to memorize so many of them."

"I just hope I didn't fail!" Darcy admitted.

Stephanie swallowed nervously. "Oh, I'm sure
you didn't *fail*," she said.

"How did *you* do, Steph?" Allie asked. "I
wonder if your test was the same as ours. What

was your first question? Was it about the tribe from Connecticut?"

Stephanie gulped. "Yeah," she said. "It was."

"What did you put?" Darcy asked. "The Pequot?"

"I wrote the Mashantucket Pequot, but I think just Pequot is okay."

Allie's frown deepened. "I put Mohegan," she said.

"They're from Connecticut, too," Stephanie told her. "So don't worry. Maybe you'll get credit."

Allie shrugged. "Who knew Ms. Cropple would ask all those tough questions?"

I knew, Stephanie thought. But there was no way she could tell her friends she had the test ahead of time. She felt too guilty about it.

Worst of all, Stephanie knew her friends would urge her to tell Ms. Cropple what happened, and she still hadn't decided if she wanted to do that. If Ms. Cropple knew someone had gotten their hands on an old test, she might make everyone take the test again.

Stephanie was sure *nobody* would like her for that.

As Stephanie listened to her friends complain about the test, her guilt gnawed at her more and more. *That's it*, she thought. *I have to find Lara and straighten this out. Fast.*

CHAPTER
10

◆ ◀ ◆ ◆

Ring . . . ring . . . ring.

Stephanie listened to the phone ring for what seemed like the hundredth time. It was her fifth call to Lara's house since school had let out for the day. For the fifth time, Stephanie got no answer.

"Arrgh!" she grumbled in frustration.

She hadn't been able to track Lara down at her school, either. Stephanie was starting to wonder if Lara was purposely avoiding her—maybe hiding from her.

There was only one option left, she realized. Lara and her group hung out at the mall pretty much every night. She'd have to hunt her down there—tonight.

Yes, Stephanie resolved. *I'll find Lara and tell her I've made a decision. I'm going to tell Ms. Cropple about having the test ahead of time.*

Stephanie realized it was all that she could do. She hoped Ms. Cropple would understand that the whole thing was just a big misunderstanding.

Michelle entered the living room, wearing a leotard and cradling Flourie in her arms. "All ready to baby-sit tonight, *Aunt* Stephanie?" she asked.

Stephanie groaned. "Michelle, I know I told you I would, but I can't take Flourie with me *tonight.* I have somewhere to go, and it will look stupid if I show up with a flour sack!"

"But all I need you to do is watch her. I have to go to my dance lesson, and I can't take Flourie with me. With all those legs flying around, she'll get stepped on!" Michelle pleaded.

"She's supposed to get a seven o'clock bottle and a seven-thirty diaper change, but I'm not going to get back from my class until at least eight o'clock. Please? No one else is around!"

Stephanie sighed. She checked the time. It was six-thirty, and she desperately needed to be at the mall by seven. She knew that was when Lara would be there.

Stephanie was about to tell her sister no, when

she noticed the look of desperation on Michelle's face. She sighed.

I guess I did promise, she thought.

"Okay, okay," Stephanie said finally. "I'll take Flourie to the mall with me."

"You'll feed her at seven?" Michelle asked.

"Yes! Don't worry!"

"And you'll change her diaper at seven-thirty? Because Mrs. Yoshida gave us a certain number of diapers and she'll know if—"

"I said I would do it, Michelle!" Stephanie grumbled. "Stop worrying already!"

Michelle smiled. She set Flourie down on the coffee table, then ran upstairs. A minute later she came down with a stuffed overnight bag.

"Okay, here's Flourie's bottle, here's a clean diaper, here are some baby wipes, and I put some powder in the bag just in case—"

"Michelle!" Stephanie cried. "Are you nuts? I can't go out with all that stuff!"

"But you have to!" Michelle insisted. "Flourie needs all these things!"

Stephanie put her head in her hands. "Look, I'll take the bottle and the diaper," she said calmly. "But she really doesn't need the rattle, the teething toy, and the change of clothes. She's a *flour* sack, Michelle!"

Michelle frowned. "Okay," she said, finally

giving in. "But promise me you'll talk to her. She likes to be cuddled and talked to."

"I promise," Stephanie said. "I'll even sing to her, okay? Now, go to your class. Joey's waiting to drive you."

Michelle sprinted toward the kitchen just as Danny entered the living room.

"Dad! What are *you* doing tonight?" Stephanie asked.

"Actually," Danny reported, "I'm going to the mall. I need to stop at Lane's for some new shoes. Mine are all worn out."

Stephanie's eyes widened. What incredible luck. "Great! That's where *I* need to go!" she exclaimed. "I'm meeting a friend from social studies there to—uh—go over our last test. Can I catch a ride with you?"

"Sure, if you're ready to go now," Danny said. "I want to be back for a TV special at nine."

"One second." Stephanie grabbed her black bag. "I'm ready!" she announced. Then she remembered Flourie. She picked up the flour sack and shoved it in her bag. Then she tossed in Flourie's bottle and diaper along with her house keys. She zipped the bag shut.

"All right, now I'm really ready," she announced. "Let's go."

* * *

91

At seven o'clock Stephanie hurried toward the bagel stand. Lara was there, along with her cheerleader friends—and Mark.

"Stephanie!" Mark said with a smile. "Cool. I didn't expect to see you here."

Stephanie smiled. "Hi, Mark," she said.

"Hi, Stephanie!" Lara said. "What's up?"

Stephanie sat on the edge of the fountain next to Lara. "Hi, I'm glad you're here," she said in a low voice. "I wanted to talk to you."

"You remember Debbie and June, right?" Lara asked.

"Hi, Stephanie!" both girls greeted her at the same time.

Stephanie smiled. "Hey, guys," she said politely. Then she turned back to Lara. "So, listen, here's what I—"

"Wait," Lara interrupted. She leaned in close so only Stephanie could hear. "Listen! I told Mark what a great help you were last night," she said quietly, "and we got to talking." She looked over her shoulder to check that Mark was out of earshot. Then she turned back to Stephanie. "He *really* likes you."

Stephanie's eyes widened. "Really? He does? What did he say exactly?" she whispered.

"He said he can't stop thinking about you," Lara told her.

Stephanie realized she couldn't prevent a smile from creeping across her face.

"Hey, what's going on?" Mark asked, stepping up to them. "Steph, you look like you just won the lottery or something."

Stephanie blushed. "Oh—uh—I was just talking to Lara about . . . school."

Mark made a face. "School?" he asked.

Luckily Lara changed the subject. "So," she said, "where did you guys decide to go on your next date?"

"I don't know," Mark replied with a shrug. "Wherever Stephanie wants to go."

"You should go to that place downtown," Lara told them. "That new doughnut shop where they make the doughnuts right in front of you. Debbie, June, and I were there last weekend. It's so much fun. And the doughnuts are great!"

June and Debbie both agreed.

"Do you want to go there, Stephanie?" Mark asked.

"Sure," she replied. "That sounds excellent."

"Hey, why don't we go for a walk? This part of the mall is awfully crowded," Mark teased.

Stephanie bit her bottom lip. She wanted to go for a walk with Mark more than anything in the whole world, but she couldn't.

Stephanie knew she *had* to talk to Lara—before she felt any worse about all of this.

"Sorry, I can't, Mark," she apologized. "I really need to talk to Lara. Privately." She turned to Lara. "Can we sit over in that booth for a sec?" she asked, pointing toward the food court.

Lara followed her to the booth. They sat across from each other.

"Listen," Stephanie began, "I've been thinking about this all day, and I think the only thing we can do to get out of this social studies mess is to tell Ms. Cropple the truth."

Lara's eyes narrowed. "Stephanie, what are you talking about? What mess?"

Stephanie stared back at her. "The test! I'm talking about the social studies test we took today!"

"That wasn't a mess," Lara argued. "We aced that test! So what's the problem?"

Stephanie looked at Lara as if she were crazy. "Of course we aced it," she said. "We had all the answers beforehand."

Lara smiled. "Right! And if it hadn't been for your help, I never would have—"

"Wait!" Stephanie cried. "Lara, I didn't mean to help you." Stephanie hesitated. "No, wait.

What I mean is, I did want to help you, but not by looking up all the answers to our test! Not by cheating!"

She took a deep breath. "Look. Here's what we have to do. We have to go to Ms. Cropple's office tomorrow morning and tell her we had the test beforehand."

Lara's eyes widened.

"It's okay!" Stephanie assured her. "Ms. Cropple is cool! She'll probably just give us a makeup exam or something. We'll just tell her the truth—that we used one of her old tests from a couple of years ago to study from, and it turned out that she reused the same test—"

Lara burst out laughing.

Stephanie stared at her in disbelief. "What's so funny?" she asked.

Lara shook her head. "I can't believe that you haven't caught on yet," she said. "I thought for sure you'd have figured it out when Cropple handed out the tests."

"What are you talking about?" Stephanie demanded. She felt herself starting to get angry.

"Stephanie," Lara said, "I didn't get that test from my cousin."

"What do you mean?" Stephanie asked. "You told me that—"

"I don't even *have* a cousin who went to my school! I made that up," Lara confessed.

"Then, where did you get the test?" Stephanie asked.

Lara leaned in close. "I got the test—this year's test—from Ms. Cropple's *desk!*"

CHAPTER
11

◆ ◀ ▶ ◆

Stephanie could not believe her ears.

"You—you mean you *stole* the test from Ms. Cropple's desk?" she stammered in disbelief.

Lara grinned proudly. "It was *so* cool. You didn't even know. You were too busy smooching with Mark!"

Stephanie's eyes widened. "You took the test when I let you into the resource room?"

Lara rolled her eyes. "Don't get so bent out of shape, Stephanie," she said. "I made two copies of it and put the original back. Cropple will never know the difference!"

Stephanie leaned back against the booth. Her head was spinning—she couldn't believe this was happening. How could she have ever left Lara alone in the resource room?

And more important, how could Lara have done this? She must have been desperate to pass, Stephanie reasoned. It was the only explanation.

"Lara," Stephanie said seriously. "You have to go to Ms. Cropple and confess everything. Sooner or later she's going to find out what happened, so I think it's better if we come clean."

Lara scoffed. "Are you out of your mind?" she asked. "No way am I confessing to Cropple."

"Lara, listen to me," Stephanie insisted, "Ms. Cropple will probably only make us take the test over. Especially if you tell her you're sorry. Trust me! I know her!"

Lara shook her head. "Stephanie, there is no way I am telling Cropple I swiped the test from her desk. She'll fail me for sure!"

Stephanie took a deep breath to calm herself. She couldn't believe what was happening.

"Lara, if you don't tell Ms. Cropple, then *I'm* going to tell her," she insisted. "I don't feel right, lying to her like this."

Lara leaned across the table, her expression suddenly cold and steely. "Stephanie, listen to me. *Nobody* is going to tell Cropple anything. And if you ever say anything to her about me taking the test from her desk, I'll totally deny it.

On top of that, I'll tell her that *you* were the one who stole the test."

Stephanie gasped. "She would never believe you!" she said.

"Yes, she would," Lara said. "I'll tell her that I went to you for some tutoring help and that you bragged about having access to all the social studies files! Not to mention the fact that you're the only student who has a key to her desk."

Stephanie wanted to kick herself for leaving Lara in the resource room alone. It was so irresponsible of her!

"Also"—Lara grinned—"I think Mark will be interested in knowing his new girlfriend is a big cheater." Lara smiled a phony smile. "Don't you agree?"

Stephanie glanced over at Mark, who was laughing with Debbie and June. She swallowed hard, reminding herself that Mark was Lara's friend long before he was hers. Mark would believe Lara's word over Stephanie's. He'd think she was a total cheater.

Stephanie held her head in her hands. How had things gone so terribly wrong? All she set out to do was help somebody.

Lara stood up. "Look, Stephanie," she said matter-of-factly, "like it or not, we're in this thing together. I say, let it go. Do nothing. Cropple will never find out, so there's no big deal. Try to be cool about this—as hard as that might be for you, okay? Now, I'm going back to hang out with my friends. Are you coming?"

Stephanie trudged back to the fountain behind Lara. She felt completely stunned. *I'm trapped,* she thought drearily. *Trapped in this terrible lie.*

As Lara and Mark and their friends chatted and laughed, Stephanie went over everything in her mind. There was no way out of the mess she was in. On the one hand, if she did nothing and just kept it between the two of them, no one would ever know the difference.

But on the other hand, Stephanie knew she couldn't deceive her teacher. Plus, now that she knew the test was stolen, there was no question about it: She *had* cheated. One hundred percent. And she couldn't ignore *that.*

Stephanie felt awful. Even after Mark put his arm around her and kissed her good-bye, she still felt terrible.

As she shuffled through the mall to meet her father, Stephanie dug into her bag for some money for a soda. When she pulled her change purse out, she noticed her hand was covered in white powder.

"What the—" Stephanie peered into her bag.

Everything was covered in white powder. There was—flour—everywhere!

Stephanie gasped. She reached into her bag and yanked Flourie out. That's when she noticed a big hole in the middle of Flourie's . . . well, her *head*, if she'd had one.

Oh, no! My keys must have ripped open the sack. I've killed Flourie!

So many things were going wrong at once that Stephanie thought she would cry. She knew her sister was going to be so upset when she found out about Flourie. But what could Stephanie do about it?

Then an idea came to her! She raced over to the Quick Mart in the mall. She searched the baking supplies aisle. Yes, Stephanie thought, they sell the same brand of flour Flourie is made of! Michelle will never know the difference!

She carried a new sack of flour to the checkout. At least the Flourie situation was fixed.

But she'd have much bigger problems to deal with at school the next day.

CHAPTER
12

◆ ◂ ▪ ◆

The next afternoon at lunch Stephanie sat in the cafeteria by herself, staring at the social studies test paper Ms. Cropple had returned that morning. She gazed at the big A+ at the top and felt sick.

A few minutes later Darcy, Allie, and Maura arrived at the table. Darcy tossed her backpack onto the floor and fell into the seat next to Stephanie.

"Can you believe it?" she asked glumly. "I got a C on my social studies test. A C! It's the lowest grade I've ever gotten on a test. And I studied so hard!"

Stephanie quickly reached for her tuna sandwich, trying to cover her test paper with her arm at the same time. She didn't want her friends to see her high grade. Especially since she hadn't earned it honestly. And she wasn't ready to explain to them what had really happened.

A moment later Allie and Maura slumped into their seats. "Maura and I both got C pluses," Allie announced unhappily. "I think all the kids in our class did poorly. It was such a hard test!"

"Well, maybe Ms. Cropple will see that nobody did well, and she won't count it in our final grade," Darcy suggested.

Allie looked hopeful. "You think?" she asked.

Maura nodded. "It's happened before," she told them. "Sometimes when all test grades are below B's, a teacher will realize the test may have been unfair."

"What do you think, Steph?" Darcy asked. "Will Ms. Cropple do that?"

Stephanie tried desperately to cover her test paper. "Oh, yeah, sure!" she said. "I've heard of that happening before." She slowly slid her bookbag over the test as she spoke. "And Ms. Cropple is usually fair when it comes to these kinds of things."

Just then Lara came bouncing up to the table.

"So, did you tell them?" she asked cheerfully.

Stephanie stared at Lara, opening her eyes as wide as possible. If Lara looked at her, maybe she'd get Stephanie's hint and not bring up the social studies test grades.

"Tell us what?" Maura asked.

"About what an excellent tutor your friend is," Lara proclaimed.

The girls all stared at Stephanie.

Lara pulled her test paper from her backpack. "B plus!" she exclaimed happily. "It's the highest mark I've ever gotten!"

Darcy's eyes narrowed. "You got a B plus?" she asked in disbelief.

"That's right!" Lara announced.

Stephanie felt sick. She knew what was coming next.

"What grade did you get, Stephanie?" Allie asked suspiciously.

"Oh, I did pretty well," Stephanie mumbled. "It was a fluke, really. That test was hard!" Stephanie glanced at the lunch table. "Hey, are you going to finish those chips?" she asked Maura, trying to change the subject.

"Show us your test," Allie demanded.

Stephanie shrugged her shoulders. She should never have tried to fool her friends, she realized. She slid the test paper out from under her backpack. She handed it to Darcy.

Darcy let out a gasp. *"Pretty well?* Stephanie, you *aced* this test!"

"Cool, huh?" Lara asked. "Stephanie is, like, the best tutor in the world!"

Stephanie glared at Lara. Then she turned back to her friends. "Listen, guys, I didn't want to tell you about my grade. Can we just drop it?"

"Why wouldn't you want us to know your grade?" Maura asked. "You did great!"

"It's not a big deal," Stephanie said.

"Yes, it is," Darcy insisted. "If you guys did well, Ms. Cropple will never dismiss this test. We're stuck with our crummy grades!"

Allie frowned. "I'm going to study every night for weeks for Ms. Cropple's next test," she said. "It's the only way I'll be able to pull up this grade."

"Well, you'd better get started," Maura told her, "because I think Ms. Cropple is giving us another test tomorrow!"

Darcy's mouth fell open. "What? So soon?" she asked in a panic. "Stephanie, is that true?"

Stephanie nodded. "I think so," she said. "Ms. Cropple has to get two exams in before the grading semester is over. But if there is a test tomorrow, it'll be a pop quiz. It couldn't be nearly as hard."

"Maybe for you," Allie remarked. "You got an A! But the rest of us had better get cracking."

Stephanie was feeling sicker by the moment.

She *really* wanted to tell her friends everything, but how could she? They'd never understand that she was tricked into cheating.

She stood up from the table and lifted her backpack. "I promised Ms. Cropple I'd help her out for a bit," she said. "So I have to go. I'll see you guys later, okay?"

Her friends nodded.

"Hey, see if you can find out if we're going to have a quiz tomorrow and what's going to be on it!" Darcy called out jokingly.

Stephanie's stomach lurched. If only Darcy knew how completely *un*funny that was.

When she got to the resource room, none of the teachers was there. Stephanie used her key and opened the door.

Inside, Ms. Cropple's desk was in its usual state of disarray. But there was a stack of papers sitting on top with a handwritten note to Stephanie.

Hi, Steph!

Great work on the exam! I'm in meetings this afternoon, so please do me a favor and check these homework assignments. Thanks!
Ms. C

Stephanie took the pile of papers over to the conference desk and began looking them over. A few minutes later there was a knock on the door.

Stephanie glanced up. Maybe it was Mark coming to pay her a visit. She looked through the little window in the door—and her heart fell. Lara stood on the other side.

Stephanie frowned and opened the door. "What do you want?" she asked, annoyed.

"What I want is in there," she said, pointing to Ms. Cropple's desk.

Stephanie's eyes narrowed. "What are you talking about?" she asked suspiciously.

"I'm talking about Cropple's next test!" Lara told her. "I want you to get it for us."

Stephanie shook her head. "No way!" she said.

Lara put her hands on her hips. "Stop being such a loser, Stephanie," she said. "What's the big deal? Haven't you ever cheated before?"

"No, as a matter of fact, I haven't," Stephanie replied.

"Well, you're making it into too big a deal," Lara went on. "We still have to do the work and look up the answers," she added.

"*We?*" Stephanie asked. "Lara, you tricked me into cheating last time. Do you think I would cheat knowingly? And do you really think I would *steal*, too?"

Lara smiled mischievously. "Yes, I think you would," she said in a drippy, sweet voice. "Especially if it meant I might spill my guts to Mark about how you stole the last test."

Stephanie's mouth fell open.

"That's right!" Lara said angrily. "If you don't get the test, I'll tell Mark everything."

Stephanie glared at her. Lara was—blackmailing her!

Lara laughed. "And don't forget, Mark's been my friend for years. He'll definitely believe me over you!"

"But I'm *not* a cheater," Stephanie insisted. She felt her face getting hot—turning bright red. "You would really lie to Mark about that . . . just so you can get this test?"

"Yes," Lara replied. "If you don't help me, you're ruining my chance at passing and staying on the cheerleading squad. And staying on the squad is more important than anything to me. More important than your relationship with Mark is to you.

"If you make sure I can't stay on the squad, I'll make sure you don't stay with Mark."

How could anyone be so mean? Stephanie wondered. *And how could I have misjudged Lara? She*

seemed so sweet and nice in the beginning. But obviously, that was all an act.

Lara had fooled her from the start, Stephanie realized. And Allie and Maura had seen right through her. Lara wasn't after Stephanie's friendship at all—she was only after Stephanie's key to Ms. Cropple's desk!

Stephanie didn't know what to do. How could she steal a test from Ms. Cropple? How could she agree to steal *anything?*

"Lara, I—" she began nervously.

"Look, you had better do this for me, and quick," Lara ordered. "I'll be waiting in the middle-school library until the end of this period. Bring me a copy of the next test—or I'll tell everyone how you stole the first test and cheated! And you can be sure Mark and Ms. Cropple will be the first two people I tell!"

CHAPTER
13

Stephanie closed the door to the resource room and locked it behind her. She stood—alone—and stared at Ms. Cropple's desk drawer. The drawer she knew contained the next social studies test.

The drawer that *she* had the key to open.

Stephanie kept staring at the drawer, thinking.

I can do this, she thought to herself, *and then be finished with Lara forever. And if I don't look at the test*, she reasoned, *maybe it won't be like I cheated.*

Stephanie fell into her chair. She knew that reasoning was totally wrong. It *would* be cheating if she stole the test for Lara.

Or, I can just refuse to do it, she thought, still staring at the desk drawer. *I can tell Lara to take a hike and that I never want to see her again.*

Of course, then I can count on never seeing Mark again, too, she reminded herself. And she really liked Mark. He was sweet, smart, and funny.

And what about Darcy? *She* was counting on Stephanie to get her in with the high school crowd. Making Mark and Lara hate her was not the way to do that.

Not to mention that if Lara went to Ms. Cropple, Stephanie would be in big trouble. Not only would she get an automatic failing grade on the test, she would lose her job in the resource room—not to mention losing Ms. Cropple's friendship and respect.

This was *so* unfair!

Stephanie felt a lump in her throat. She glanced at the clock on the wall and thought about Lara, waiting for her in the library.

Waiting for Stephanie to slip her the stolen test.

Stephanie had only a few minutes to make a decision. Steal the test, or deal with Lara lying to everyone she knew.

Stephanie pulled the keys from her pocket and unlocked the drawer. She rifled through Ms.

Cropple's files until she found what she was looking for. Her heart beat wildly.

The door to the resource room flew open.

"Stephanie? What are you doing?"

Stephanie spun around. Oh, no! It was Ms. Cropple!

"I . . . I . . ." Stephanie could barely get the words out. Out of the corner of her eye she saw what looked like tomorrow's quiz sticking out of a file. What if Ms. Cropple saw it? She'd know Stephanie had been going to steal it!

Stephanie cleared her throat and forced herself to speak. "Um, I was just organizing your files for you," she said, thinking quickly. She pulled the test out of the drawer and mixed it with some other papers she was holding.

"I was looking for that homework answer key to grade those papers you wanted, and I noticed your files were out of order."

Ms. Cropple grinned. "I can't believe how organized you are!" she exclaimed. "I swear, Stephanie, if you weren't helping me this semester, I would be buried in paperwork!"

Stephanie managed another smile. But inside, she was cringing. "Oh, no problem," she said. "I like working with you." She paused. "So, what are you doing here, anyway? I thought you had a class this period."

112

Ms. Cropple walked over to her bookcase. "I do!" she said. "I forgot one of the books I needed for today's lesson."

Stephanie held the test close to her chest as she watched Ms. Cropple search the bookcase. Finally, Ms. Cropple found the book she was looking for.

"Here it is!" the teacher said, and then headed for the door. "Keep up the good work, Steph!" Ms. Cropple walked out of the resource room, the door closing behind her.

Stephanie felt totally sick. What was she doing? How could she have turned into such a horrible person? Someone who cheats and lies—and steals?

Still clutching the stolen quiz, Stephanie ran out of the resource room.

Lara was waiting for her by the copy machine in the library. When she saw the papers in Stephanie's hands, she smiled.

"Way to go, Steph!" she exclaimed. "I knew you would come through for me."

Stephanie thrust the test at Lara. "Here's the deal," she said angrily. "This is *it*! I'm calling the shots now. This is the last time I'm doing something like this for you. Don't ask me to again, because I won't! Consider us even."

Lara quickly made two copies of the test and gave the original back to Stephanie. "Deal!" she said. "This should be enough to bring up my grade so I don't fail the semester, anyway. So, we're even! Here's your copy."

Stephanie stared at her in disbelief. "*My* copy?" she asked. "I don't want a copy of the test! I'm not going to cheat!"

Lara made a face. "Oh, come on, Stephanie! Don't be a Goody Two-Shoes! Take the test! You've already done the hard part!"

Stephanie shook her head. Lara just didn't get it. She pulled her backpack onto her shoulder and walked out of the library. She headed back to the resource room to return the test to Ms. Cropple's desk drawer.

She was down the hall, when she felt a clap on her back. Stephanie spun around.

"What do you want, Lara?" she demanded.

"Look," Lara said, "I just wanted to say thanks. I know this was hard for you. But I *need* to see this test. I can't fail social studies. I just can't."

"Fine," Stephanie snapped. "But there are other ways of passing, you know. Like *studying*. You should try it sometime."

"It's too late for that now," Lara countered.

"Look, you do what you have to do. But from now on I want no part of it." She paused. "In fact, I don't think I want any part of *you*, either, Lara."

"No problem," Lara countered. "From now on, you can consider us *ex*-friends."

CHAPTER
14

◆ ◀ ◆ ◆

Stephanie walked into the kitchen, feeling awful. She poured herself a glass of milk. Then paused mid-sip as she heard a sniffling sound behind her.

She turned and saw Michelle sitting at the kitchen table, close to tears. "Michelle, what's wrong?" Stephanie asked.

"I got disqualified," she replied sadly. "Disqualified from getting the Best Parent award."

Stephanie put down her glass. "You *what?* But you were such a good parent! You loved Flourie like a baby. How could Mrs. Yoshida disqualify you?"

Stephanie felt terrible for her sister. As stupid

as the whole flour baby thing had been, she finally accepted that Michelle was really serious about it.

Michelle shrugged sadly. "Mrs. Yoshida said Flourie wasn't the same flour sack that I got at the beginning of the assignment," she explained. "But that can't be. I never switched Flourie. I took care of her fair and square!"

Stephanie gasped. She felt her heart skip a beat. "Wait," she said. "Mrs. Yoshida thinks you replaced Flourie with another sack of flour?"

"Uh-huh," Michelle replied. "But I didn't. I swear!" Michelle ran out of the kitchen and upstairs to her room.

Stephanie fell into a chair. *How could Mrs. Yoshida have possibly known I bought a new bag of flour?* she wondered. *There was no way to tell. I bought the exact same brand! The bags were identical!*

D.J. came into the kitchen a moment later. "What's the matter with Michelle?" she asked worriedly. "She's locked herself in her room and won't open the door. Do you know what happened?"

Stephanie sighed. "Yeah, I know what happened. And I think it's my fault."

D.J. frowned, puzzled. "Huh? How?" she asked. "What happened?"

"It happened last night at the mall. See, I took

117

Flourie with me because I promised Michelle I would baby-sit. But when I stuffed Flourie in my pouch purse—"

"You stuffed Flourie in your bag?" D.J. asked in horror.

Stephanie made a face. "Deej, we're talking about a sack of flour, remember? Anyway, I threw my keys into my bag right after, and I guess they punctured Flourie in her head."

D.J. grimaced. "Ouch!"

"I know," Stephanie agreed, shuddering. "So anyway, I went into the Quick Mart and bought another bag of flour."

"You did *what?*" D.J. asked.

"I replaced Flourie with a new sack of flour," Stephanie explained. "And Mrs. Yoshida disqualified Michelle for cheating."

D.J. shook her head. "Oh, Stephanie."

"I only did it to *help* Michelle!" Stephanie insisted. "I knew she'd be upset, so I didn't tell her I switched Flourie. You see, Michelle didn't really cheat."

"Stephanie," D.J. began. "Mrs. Yoshida's flour baby project was important. It was supposed to teach Michelle how to take good care of living things. I know Flourie wasn't living and breathing, but Michelle's job was to treat her as if she were. If you punctured Flourie while you were watching her, you should have told Michelle. Sure, she would have been upset, but she could have fixed Flourie. Instead, *you* cheated."

Stephanie cringed at her sister's words. It seemed as if she were cheating all the time lately.

"I am *sooo* sorry," she told D.J.

"Don't tell me," D.J. said. "Tell Michelle."

"I will," Stephanie resolved. "And I'm going to tell Mrs. Yoshida, too. When she hears what really happened, maybe she won't disqualify Michelle."

Yes, Stephanie thought. She'd apologize to Michelle and set Mrs. Yoshida straight. That would fix everything.

If only her situation with Lara had such an easy solution!

Michelle sat on her bed in a daze. "You killed Flourie and then thought you could buy a new one?" she asked Stephanie in amazement.

"Well, yes," Stephanie replied.

"But Mrs. Yoshida *numbered* all the flour sacks!" Michelle cried. "Did you put a number on Flourie?"

Stephanie grimaced. "No. I didn't know the number was there. So I didn't put a number on the new sack. That's probably how Mrs. Yoshida knew Flourie had been replaced.

"I'm *really* sorry, Michelle," Stephanie added. "So I'm going to see Mrs. Yoshida for you and explain that I was the one who cheated all those times."

Michelle raised her eyes. "Huh? *All* those times? What do you mean?" she asked. "You switched Flourie more than once?"

Stephanie shook her head. "No, Michelle. But some of those other things I did—like checking Flourie's chart even if you didn't change her or feed her—that was kind of cheating, too."

"You mean I was cheating the whole time?" Michelle asked.

Stephanie nodded. "Sort of," she said.

Michelle sprawled out on her bed. "So I don't deserve the Best Parent award anyway," she said sadly.

"That's not true, Michelle," Stephanie told her sister. "You were a great parent to Flourie. You loved her and took really good care of her. I was the one who was wrong here. I thought your project was, well, silly. So I didn't give you the best advice about it. And I didn't take extra special care of Flourie." She sat next to Michelle on the bed.

"I was totally wrong. Everything was my

fault. Cheating a little bit is still cheating," she added, thinking of Lara as well. "I'll explain everyting to Mrs. Yoshida. And I'll even baby-sit for Flourie Two if you want, okay? I'll sing to her and everything."

"Forget it," Michelle grumbled. "If I need a baby-sitter, I'll ask Dad. He's more responsible! *He* never punctured any of us kids in the head with keys!"

"Ouch!" Stephanie laughed. "I guess I deserved that. So—do you forgive me?"

"I guess so," Michelle said. "As long as you explain to Mrs. Yoshida what happened."

"Thanks, Michelle." Stephanie gave her sister a hug. "I'll make everything up to you. I promise."

"It's okay, Stephanie. After all, she was only a sack of flour!" Michelle smiled. She jumped off her bed and left the room.

Stephanie shook her head. Then she went over to her own bed and spread her social studies notes all around her. *Yikes! I have a lot of reading to do for tomorrow's quiz*, she realized.

She reached into her backpack for another book, when a folded piece of paper slipped out and onto her bed.

Stephanie stared at it. She picked it up off the

bed and unfolded it. To her horror, it was a copy of the next day's quiz!

"Lara must have sneaked it into my bag when we were in the hallway," she cried out in disgust. Stephanie stared at the test. She was furious!

Stephanie tore the test paper in half, then tossed the pieces into the wastepaper basket.

Lara had some nerve! Just because *she* was a liar and a cheater didn't mean Stephanie had to be one, too.

Well, there's no way I'm going to cheat on tomorrow's test! Stephanie thought to herself. *I wouldn't even care if Lara had filled out the answers before slipping this into my bag! There is no way I'm going to give another look at the stolen paper!*

Stephanie went back to her social studies notes. As she began studying, something nagged at the back of her mind. Something about the way that test paper had looked. There was something strange about it.

She stood and walked over to the wastepaper basket. She picked up the test-paper pieces and smoothed them out on her bed. At first glance something had seemed odd. . . .

Stephanie read the first two questions. Then she felt a huge grin spread across her face. Her smile soon turned into a laugh, and suddenly she was laughing like crazy.

"This is too good to be true." She laughed out loud to herself.

A moment ago she was dreading the social studies quiz.

But now she couldn't wait to take it!

CHAPTER
15

The next morning Stephanie sat at her desk in social studies. She was a little tired from having stayed up late studying, but she was eager for Ms. Cropple to hand out the quizzes.

Ms. Cropple stood in the front of the room, holding the quizzes in her arms.

"Before I pass out today's quiz," she announced, "I have some news. It has come to my attention that my last exam may have been too difficult. Therefore, I have decided not to count those grades in your overall averages."

There was a gasp from a few of the students, but Stephanie gazed around the room and thought that most of her classmates seemed relieved and happy.

A lot of kids must have scored pretty low, she thought to herself. Secretly, Stephanie was happy that the test wasn't going to be included in her grade point average. Now maybe she could forget about that test entirely!

Ms. Cropple handed out the quizzes. Before beginning, Stephanie glanced in Lara's direction. Lara was obviously upset about the grade on the last test not counting.

Stephanie watched as Ms. Cropple handed that day's quiz to Lara. She couldn't wait to see Lara's face when Lara read the first question!

Stephanie turned sideways in her chair and observed Lara out of the corner of her eye. Lara smiled as she picked up her pencil. Then she began to read. Slowly her face fell. She frantically flipped the test over and scanned the back. Her eyes were filled with panic. Her head jerked up. She shot an angry look at Stephanie.

But Stephanie turned back in her seat and smiled to herself. She picked up her pencil and began to write.

Stephanie finished her quiz one minute before the bell rang. Luckily, it wasn't difficult because she had made sure she was well prepared.

She handed in the quiz, stepped into the hallway, and headed for her locker.

She felt someone grip her shoulder. She spun around and found herself face-to-face with Lara.

"You did that on purpose. You gave me the wrong test!" Lara cried angrily. Her face was red, and her mouth trembled as she spoke.

"Actually, no," Stephanie told her. "At first I thought I'd given you the right test. But later, when I looked at the copy you put in my bag, I saw that it was the wrong test. The test I took from Ms. Cropple's desk was on the Inuit Indians. We haven't even started studying them yet!"

"How could you not tell me?" Lara fumed. "I spent all night studying the wrong chapters!"

"Studying?" Stephanie asked sarcastically. "Is that what you call it? Well, I call it cheating. And cheating is something I don't do!"

"You're finished, Stephanie!" Lara yelled in Stephanie's face. "I'm going to drag your name through the mud! I'm going to tell Mark and Cropple—and both schools that you are a cheater. I'm telling everyone that you stole two tests from Cropple's desk!"

Stephanie kept on smiling. "Do what you want," she said calmly. "But there's something you should know."

Lara's eyes narrowed. "What?" she snapped.

"It's too late!" Stephanie told her. "I've already told Ms. Cropple *everything!*"

Lara's face went white. "What?"

"I told her," Stephanie said again. "Early this morning. I told her how you did all this just to stay on the cheerleading squad, and how you threatened to frame me. That's why Ms. Cropple decided to discount the test entirely."

Lara opened her mouth to say something, but at the same second Ms. Cropple poked her head out of the classroom.

"Lara Tempkin?" she said. "Come back into the classroom, please. We need to discuss something."

Stephanie watched as Lara hung her head and stepped into the room. For a brief moment Stephanie didn't feel mad at Lara.

She just felt very sorry for her.

CHAPTER
16

◆ ◀ ◢ ◆

"Hey, Steph!" Darcy jogged over to Stephanie at the bus stop. "I've been looking all over for you. Where have you been?"

Stephanie smiled. "I've been looking all over for *you*," she said. "How was your quiz?"

"A piece of cake!" Darcy replied. "And did you hear? Cropple isn't counting the last test. Too many kids did poorly."

"I know," Stephanie told her. "And by the way, you have *me* to thank for that."

"What are we thanking you for?" Allie asked. She and Maura strolled up beside Stephanie.

Stephanie grinned. "Well, you wouldn't believe what I've been through this past week!

At least now I can finally tell you guys about it!''

Stephanie's friends exchanged glances.

"What are you talking about?" Darcy asked.

"Well," Stephanie began, "it seems Allie and Maura were right about Lara Tempkin all along."

Allie and Maura looked at each other. "We were?" they asked.

Stephanie nodded. "Yup. She didn't become my friend because she liked me—she only wanted someone to help her cheat on her social studies tests!"

"Get out of here. Really?" Maura asked.

"That's right. She actually *stole* our last big test from Ms. Cropple's desk. Then she convinced me to study from it by pretending it was an old test of Ms. Cropple's that her cousin had given her."

The girls gazed at Stephanie, stunned.

"That's why Lara and I did so well on that test the other day. Because we knew all the questions ahead of time," Stephanie explained.

Darcy gasped. "You—*cheated?*"

Stephanie sighed. "Yes—but not on purpose," she added. "I had no idea that the test we were studying from was really the test we were going to take the next day. And once I found out, I was fuming!

"Then," Stephanie went on, "Lara tried to blackmail me. She said if I didn't steal today's quiz for her, she'd tell Mark and Ms. Cropple and everyone at both the middle and high schools that it was *me* who stole all the tests and cheated."

"This is unbelievable!" Darcy exclaimed.

"It sounds like a soap opera," Maura agreed.

"At first I didn't know what to do. So I took the quiz from Ms. Cropple's desk and gave it to Lara. I hoped it would make her leave me alone. But later on I realized that I took the wrong quiz! I didn't tell Lara, and she studied from it. She looked up the answers to all the wrong questions!"

"No way!" Allie cracked up.

"Really—that's what happened!" Stephanie said. "Anyway I came clean with Ms. Cropple this morning. I told her everything, and she said she was wondering why Lara and I were the only ones with good grades on the test. Once I told her it was because we had the questions beforehand, she decided not to count the test scores at all."

"Was Ms. Cropple mad at you?" Darcy asked.

"Majorly," Stephanie admitted. "But we worked

it out. I have to work in the resource room a couple of extra hours to make up for it all. But I don't mind that part," she added.

"Whoa!" Allie shook her head in disbelief. "Why didn't you tell us about any of this?" she asked.

"I wanted to," Stephanie said, "but I felt so guilty, I just couldn't. And then, when you guys got low grades, I thought you'd be mad at me if I told you I'd known the answers ahead of time."

Maura laughed. "We probably *would* have been a little mad!" she said.

"I wouldn't have blamed you," Stephanie said. "But I wanted to work things out on my own."

"What about you and Mark?" Darcy asked.

"Funny you should mention Mark," Allie whispered. "He's headed toward us right now!"

Stephanie turned just as Mark reached them.

"Uh—Stephanie, can I talk to you in private for a second?" he asked.

This is it, Stephanie thought. *He knows what happened. And now he's going to break up with me.*

She glanced at her friends, then followed Mark a few paces away from the bus stop.

"So, you heard about what happened with me and Lara?" she asked.

131

Mark nodded. "Debbie DiAngelo just told me," he said. "Lara's off the squad."

Stephanie gulped. *Here it comes,* she thought. *He's going to break up with me now.* She braced herself for the blow.

"I told her cheating was a bad idea, but she insisted on doing it anyway." Mark shook his head.

Stephanie nearly fell over. "Huh? Did you just say you knew Lara was cheating?"

"Sure." Mark nodded. "Stephanie, we're best friends. Lara told me all about it." He cleared his throat. "Anyway, she thought that with you involved, there was no way she'd get caught stealing the tests, but I guess—"

"Wait a minute," Stephanie interrupted. "You knew Lara was trying to make me steal the tests from Ms. Cropple's desk, and you didn't even try to warn me?"

"I didn't know *what* to do," Mark admitted. "But I have to say, Stephanie, I can't blame you for turning Lara in. I mean, cheating is one thing, but stealing is another."

Stephanie stared at Mark. She felt completely dumbfounded.

"So, what I'm trying to say, Stephanie, is that even though this whole thing with Lara got really messed up, I still like you. And I still want to go out with you this weekend." He paused. "What do you think? Do you still want to go?"

Stephanie felt her heart sink. She had liked Mark—a lot, but she couldn't believe he was so dishonest.

She gazed at his face. His green eyes didn't seem to have quite the same sparkle. His dimples weren't nearly so cute as she thought they were.

"Stephanie," Mark repeated. "Do you still want to go out this weekend?"

Stephanie stared directly into Mark's eyes. "No way, Mark. Not if you were the last date on earth."

She left Mark to rejoin her friends.

"What happened?" Darcy whispered as soon as Stephanie was close enough to hear.

"Guess what? Mark knew Lara planned to cheat all along," Stephanie informed them.

"No way!" Maura's eyes went wide.

"It's true. He told me he knew all about her plan. Then he asked me if I wanted to go out this weekend," Stephanie said.

"And . . ." Darcy nudged Stephanie.

"What did you say?" Allie asked.

Stephanie smiled at her friends. "Let's just say that that was one question I didn't have to cheat to know the answer to!"

FULL HOUSE™
Michelle

#5: THE GHOST IN MY CLOSET 53573-0/$3.99

#6: BALLET SURPRISE 53574-9/$3.99

#7: MAJOR LEAGUE TROUBLE 53575-7/$3.99

#8: MY FOURTH-GRADE MESS 53576-5/$3.99

#9: BUNK 3, TEDDY, AND ME 56834-5/$3.99

#10: MY BEST FRIEND IS A MOVIE STAR!
(Super Edition) 56835-3/$3.99

#11: THE BIG TURKEY ESCAPE 56836-1/$3.99

#12: THE SUBSTITUTE TEACHER 00364-X/$3.99

#13: CALLING ALL PLANETS 00365-8/$3.99

#14: I'VE GOT A SECRET 00366-6/$3.99

#15: HOW TO BE COOL 00833-1/$3.99

#16: THE NOT-SO-GREAT OUTDOORS 00835-8/$3.99

#17: MY HO-HO-HORRIBLE CHRISTMAS 00836-6/$3.99

MY AWESOME HOLIDAY FRIENDSHIP BOOK
(An Activity Book) 00840-4/$3.99

FULL HOUSE MICHELLE OMNIBUS 02181-8/$6.99

#18: MY ALMOST PERFECT PLAN 00837-4/$3.99

#19: APRIL FOOLS 01729-2/$3.99

A MINSTREL® BOOK
Published by Pocket Books

Simon & Schuster Mail Order Dept. BWB
200 Old Tappan Rd., Old Tappan, N.J. 07675

Please send me the books I have checked above. I am enclosing $_____ (please add $0.75 to cover the
postage and handling for each order. Please add appropriate sales tax). Send check or money order–no cash or C.O.D.'s please. Allow up to
six weeks for delivery. For purchase over $10.00 you may use VISA: card number, expiration date and customer signature must be included.

Name _____

Address _____

City _____ State/Zip _____

VISA Card # _____ Exp.Date _____

Signature _____

1033-26

FULL HOUSE™
SISTERS

A brand-new series starring Stephanie AND Michelle!

#1 Two On The Town

Stephanie and Michelle find themselves
in the big city—and in big trouble!

(Coming in mid-November 1998)

#2 One Boss Too Many

Stephanie and Michelle think camp will be major fun.
If only these two sisters were getting along!

(Coming in mid-December 1998)

When sisters get together...expect the unexpected!

A MINSTREL® BOOK

Published by Pocket Books

2012